"Do you know how many times in the past four years I've awakened in the night to find myself reaching for you?" Damon asked.

Cory inhaled sharply as his hands slipped beneath her blouse and began caressing her. His green eyes glittered when she arched her back in sensual response.

"Did you think about me too?" he asked. "Maybe not, but you're thinking now, aren't you, Cory?"

She could think of nothing else as his hands roamed over her body, exploring, playing, toying, stroking until she thought she'd go up in flames. Her teeth bit into her lower lip to keep back the moan that trembled in her throat.

"No, don't make a sound." Damon's eyes were blazing now, his nostrils flaring. "I don't want anyone to hear the little cries you make when I'm loving you. They're mine, just as you're mine."

"No, I'm not—" She broke off as he pulled her fiercely against him and she felt her body respond to his. Heat. Shock. Hunger.

"You are mine. Always." His voice held an intensity that stunned her "You were mine then, and you're mine now. . . ."

WHAT ARE *LOVESWEPT* ROMANCES?

They are stories of true romance and touching emotion. We believe those two very important ingredients are constants in our highly sensual and very believable stories in the *LOVESWEPT* line. Our goal is to give you, the reader, stories of consistently high quality that may sometimes make you laugh, sometimes make you cry, but are always fresh and creative and contain many delightful surprises within their pages.

Most romance fans read an enormous number of books. Those they truly love, they keep. Others may be traded with friends and soon forgotten. We hope that each *LOVESWEPT* romance will be a treasure—a "keeper." We will always try to publish

LOVE STORIES YOU'LL NEVER FORGET
BY AUTHORS YOU'LL ALWAYS REMEMBER

The Editors

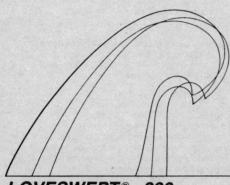

LOVESWEPT® • 280

Iris Johansen
Strong, Hot Winds

 BANTAM BOOKS
TORONTO • NEW YORK • LONDON • SYDNEY • AUCKLAND

STRONG, HOT WINDS

A Bantam Book / September 1988

If you would be interested in receiving protective vinyl covers for your Loveswept books, please write to this address for information:

Loveswept
Bantam Books
P.O. Box 985
Hicksville, NY 11802

ISBN 0-553-21919-7

Published simultaneously in the United States and Canada

PRINTED IN THE UNITED STATES OF AMERICA

O   0 9 8 7 6 5 4 3 2 1

One

"Did you find her?" Selim asked as Damon was stepping out of the jeep. Then, as Damon took off his hat to wipe his brow, Selim had his answer; it was in the bleakness of Damon's expression, the emptiness of his eyes.

"Too late," Damon said wearily. He snapped his fingers. The driver of the jeep pressed on the accelerator and the vehicle took off toward the garage across the courtyard. "She was already dead," he muttered, closing his eyes. "So small. Dear God, she was so tiny lying there in the sand. I never want to see anything like that again."

"Perhaps you won't have to," Selim said gently. "Perhaps it won't happen again."

Damon's lids lifted to reveal eyes that glittered with moist brilliance. "And perhaps it will, if I take no action. Perhaps there will be another life thrown away as if it had no value."

Selim hesitated, wanting to give comfort and yet knowing there was none he could give. What Damon said was true. He was the only one who could prevent another death, but the effort to do so might cause him even more pain than he was experiencing now. "Did you render judgment?"

"No." Damon gazed out at the shifting dunes of the Sedikhan desert that were now painted blood-red by the rays of the setting sun. The sky was blood-red too. It was as if the entire world were covered in blood, Damon thought numbly.

"Damon, you *have* to render judgment."

Damon whirled to face him. "Do you think I don't know that?" he asked harshly. "But not *now*, dammit. I keep seeing—" He turned abruptly and climbed the steps leading to the palace. "I'll wait. Raban isn't going anyplace. Marain says the tribe will be content to stay put right now. I need to get away and try to get some perspective."

"But you know even now what your judgment will be."

"True. However, I don't have to give it. Not yet." An edge of desperation mixed with the weariness and pain in Damon's voice. "Not yet."

Selim caught up with Damon as he reached the front door. "Not yet," he agreed quietly. "But soon."

Damon paused before the twelve-foot double doors, the crimson light illuminating the strong, almost brutal planes of his face. "Soon."

A servant threw open the brass-studded mahogany doors and they entered the mosaic-tiled foyer.

Damon rubbed the back of his neck to ease the tension constricting the muscles. "Dear Lord, I'm tired. I feel as if part of me drained out and into the sand back there."

"Go to bed. There's nothing important you have to attend to before . . ." Selim's words trailed off. "Damn! I forgot about Updike. He arrived this morning and has been waiting to see you. Do you want me to put him off?"

"What's it about?"

"He wouldn't tell me." Selim shrugged. "But he says it's important enough to warrant the bonus you pay for special information."

Damon grimaced. "Then I guess I'd better see him."

"Now?"

"There's no need to make myself particularly presentable," Damon said sardonically. "Updike's not very good at hiding his belief that I'm something of a barbarian. Give me ten minutes to splash some water in my face and fix myself a cool drink. Then bring him to the library."

Selim nodded and started to turn away.

"Thanks, Selim."

Selim glanced back over his shoulder. "For what?"

"For not reminding me of my duty."

"Why should I rake you over the coals when you do such a good job yourself?" Selim asked lightly.

"I just give thanks every day that I'm not the sheikh of the El Zabor." He started down the long hallway.

"The sheikh will see you now." Selim Abol made a face. "But there had better be something damn interesting in that briefcase you're carrying. He's not in a very good mood at the moment and might prove difficult."

"When isn't he difficult?" Updike asked sourly as he followed the slim young assistant down the gleaming corridor. "I've gotten used to him."

"Have you indeed?" Selim murmured, glancing back over his shoulder with distinctly skeptical eyes. "But then, you've never seen him in a really bad mood. As I recall, he's been very patient in his dealings with you, Updike."

"Patient?" Raymond Updike's tone was incredulous. "If you call it patient to demand we gather information in one day that generally takes weeks . . ."

"The sheikh pays you exorbitant amounts to get the information he needs." There was a hint of steel in Selim's tone. "Your detective agency has profited enormously in the last few years and he's asked relatively little of you—only that you keep an eye on certain unstable personnel in his companies and occasionally investigate some of the sleight of hand going on in the stock market. He just doesn't like to wait."

"I know that." Updike was suddenly conciliatory. "I didn't mean to be critical of Sheikh El

Karim. It was a long flight from New York, and I guess I'm tired."

"So is the sheikh. He just drove in from one of the El Zabor encampments and hasn't slept for forty-eight hours." Selim again glanced down at Updike's briefcase. "As I said, it had better be interesting."

"It will be," Updike said confidently. "Do you think I would have flown halfway around the world if I hadn't believed it would be worth my while?"

"No, which is the reason I'm letting you see him before he rests." Selim paused before an elaborately carved door and smiled faintly. "But if I find you've had me disturb him for nothing, you're going to wish you'd never heard of Kasmara."

Silky menace shimmered beneath the softness of Selim's voice and caused Updike to shudder. Lord, he thought, for an instant he had actually been afraid of this handsome kid who looked more like an elegant male model than an executive assistant. He had met Abol only twice before and both times had been in the presence of the sheikh, a very commanding man. He should have paid more attention to Selim. Now that he could judge Selim on his own merits, he wasn't sure he liked what he saw. The young man's easy charm and good humor appeared to be a mere front to hide an underlying hardness and his smile held an element of ferocity. He had seen that same fierce protectiveness in the other servants and followers of the sheikh, but he had assumed Abol was too westernized to be fanatically devoted to El Karim.

It seemed he had been mistaken. Selim was obviously ready to tear him apart if he wasted the time of his precious employer.

"He won't be disappointed," Updike said before frowning impatiently. "Now, can I see him?"

Selim opened the door and entered the library ahead of him. "Updike. Will you need me, or shall I go make those calls to Marasef?"

"Stay. This won't take long." Damon leaned back in the big executive chair and propped his dusty brown boots on the mahogany desk, crossing his legs at the ankle. His cool green gaze fastened on the detective. "Will it, Updike?"

"Not long at all," Updike assured him quickly as he came into the room and shut the door. "I understand you're tired and I'll make this as brief as possible." He came forward and laid his briefcase on the desk. He noticed with distaste that the sheikh looked even more like a brigand than usual. His khaki shirt was sweat-stained in places, his dark curly hair rumpled, and he smelled of brandy. He'd probably been out carousing for the two days that Updike had been forced to cool his heels here at the palace waiting for him. "You *did* say there would be a bonus for any information you found of real interest."

"You could have phoned it in," Damon said dryly. "I suppose you're planning on billing me for the flight from New York?"

"Only if you find the information is worth it." Updike's tone was smooth. "But I'm not worried."

Damon gazed at him with narrowed eyes. "What's this all about? The IBM stock purchase?"

Updike shook his head. "It's in regard to the Brandel surveillance."

Unreadable emotion flicked across Damon's face and was gone almost before Updike registered it. "I doubt if any news regarding that particular matter would warrant a bonus. I ordered a very casual surveillance of Cory Brandel."

"Casual" surveillance, Updike thought cynically, meant to the sheikh the unearthing of every detail of the woman's personal and professional life. Yet, Updike reminded himself, he, too, had considered the surveillance casual until he had run across one choice bit of information. "Bear with me," he said, drawing out a large manila envelope from his briefcase. He placed it on the desk in front of the sheikh and then took out a black videotape box. "May I use your videotape recorder?"

The sheikh nodded. "Selim."

Selim took the videotape from Updike and crossed to the media center on the far wall of the library.

"You understand this information would have turned up much sooner if you'd asked for an investigative report instead of merely a surveillance," Updike said.

Damon shrugged. "It was really only a whim that led me to order the surveillance. Cory Brandel is nothing to me."

"Right." Updike carefully kept any hint of irony

from his tone. "Still, I think you will find this tape interesting."

Damon glanced down at the envelope on the desk and his hands tightened with unconscious force on the arms of the chair. "I'm not interested in seeing the woman in bed with Koenig, if that's what you call a scoop. It's nothing to me whom she sleeps with, so if one of your men planted a camera in Koenig's bedroom, you can take your obscene little tape and shove it."

"Koenig isn't involved in this matter. I don't think he even knows about it." Updike was experiencing a spurt of excitement. "She's kept this very confidential. It's really amazing how she's managed a successful career as a television news correspondent and still— But you'll see for yourself."

"If you ever decide to show me," Damon said caustically.

Selim crossed back across the room and handed the remote control to Updike before dropping onto the visitor's chair beside the desk. "Just press the play button."

"In a moment," Updike said. He was beginning to enjoy the prospect of rocking the sheikh off his high horse. "I'd like to review the history of the surveillance so you'll better understand why we didn't—"

"For heaven's sake, get on with it," Damon said wearily.

"As you know, we began the surveillance three years ago, and had no problem. Miss Brandel leads an exceptionally open life. She works very hard at her job and travels extensively. She does have this one relationship with a fellow reporter, Gary Keonig."

"I know that," Damon snapped. "It was in your reports."

"Yes, and so were her frequent visits to her friend Bettina Langstrom in Meadowpark, Connecticut. She seemed to spend every free moment there. We didn't find it surprising she enjoyed being in the Langstrom home. Carter and Bettina Langstrom seem to be your average attractive, outgoing couple with two children, a three-year-old station wagon, and a thirty-year mortgage. It probably was a great relief for Miss Brandel to visit the Langstroms and get away from a career as fraught with tension as hers."

"Is this leading somewhere?" Damon asked impatiently.

"Yes." Updike smiled. "We're moving right along. Where was I? Oh, yes, the Langstroms. Carter Langstrom was the manager of a textile mill until a few years ago, when it shut down. Since then he's had a number of supervisory positions, none of them as lucrative as the one he had in the plant that shut down." Then, as Updike noticed Damon's impatience increasing, he hurried on. "I'm not meandering. This all has bearing."

"Get to the bare bones," Damon ordered tersely.

"Just one more item. It's the custom of our agency to make a superficial study of our clients."

Damon's position didn't change, but his muscles tensed as if readying to spring. "Are you saying you investigated *me*?" he asked softly.

"Nothing confidential," Updike said hurriedly. "Just a general profile so that we could serve your needs better. But there were pictures in the file. . ." Updike trailed off as he met Damon's gaze. He'd better move quickly or the damn savage would probably have his head lopped off. He wouldn't put it past him. He hurriedly pressed the play button on the remote control. "I was leafing through the file the other day and ran across the pictures, and something clicked."

"Clicked?" The sheikh's voice was ominously cold.

"I made a connection. I'd had some videotapes made at the Langstroms at a Sunday barbecue and—"

"Home movies?" Damon asked sardonically.

The static on the television screen suddenly cleared and Updike gave a sigh of relief. "There's Miss Brandel sitting on the grass talking to Bettina Langstrom."

"I know what she looks like," Damon said.

So did Updike, but he still found it a pleasure to gaze at Cory Brandel. Her face had always held a fascination for him as well as for millions of TV viewers. Her jawline was too long and her lips too full to be considered classically beautiful. Yet those lips were both sensitive and exquisitely formed and her enormous brown eyes sparkled with vitality and intelligence.

"She's too thin," Damon said abruptly. "Has she been ill?"

"No, but she just got back from another trip to Nicaragua. She may have lost a few pounds down there."

"A few! She's lost at least fifteen pounds. She wasn't that thin when—" Damon broke off, gazing even more intently at the woman on the screen. The strong sunlight shone on Cory Brandel's ash-blond hair, highlighting the streaks threading the mop of wild, careless curls that fell almost to her shoulders. "And her hair was longer and smoother."

"She's worn it like that for over two years."

Damon was silent, his gaze fixed on the television screen. She had changed in other ways, he thought. The nervous vitality and restlessness that had charged her every movement were still present but seemed more under her control now. There was a new maturity about her. Before she had sparkled, now she shimmered. He could feel the tension building within him and he quickly blocked it. Hell no, not again. "Updike, I don't—"

"Here," Updike interrupted, pointing. "This is the part I intended you to see. The kid . . ."

A dark-haired little boy had thrown himself into Cory Brandel's arms and was chattering excitedly to her. Cory was laughing at him as she pulled him onto her lap and rocked him back and forth, nodding every now and then as she listened.

The restlessness had suddenly vanished from Cory's face and it was radiant with affection. It was a moment before Damon could pull his gaze away. "So she's fond of children," he said gruffly.

"No, didn't you notice?" Updike zeroed in on the child's face and froze the frame.

Black curly hair, green eyes alight with boyish mischief, and a bone structure that was familiar.

Selim let out an astonished sigh.

"I took the liberty of collating this shot with one of the pictures I found in your file." Updike pressed the button and two pictures appeared on the screen. "I chose one of the shots of you at about the same age, Sheikh El Karim. It's black and white, so I'll just tune out the color."

"Almost identical," Selim said. His gaze flew to Damon's face. "Dear Lord, Damon, he's—"

"My son," Damon finished slowly, his gaze transfixed by the two pictures on the screen.

"I didn't think you knew," Updike said with satisfaction. "At first I thought that was why you had Miss Brandel under surveillance, but then I realized you'd probably have asked to have the child under similar surveillance. I thought you'd want me to make a definite verification, but that didn't prove possible. There are additional photographs and a copy of the birth certificate in that envelope, but you won't find anything you can use in a court of law. Oh, we could prove that only the little girl was Bettina Langstrom's child and that the boy was born to Cory Brandel. But there was no father's name listed on the birth certificate."

Damon's gaze never left the screen.

"Miss Brandel accepted a newsroom assignment for the last five months of her pregnancy. Then after the baby was born she resumed her job as a television reporter. The child lives with the Langstroms and appears very happy and well cared for. Miss Brandel pays the monthly mortgage on the Langstroms' home and gives them money for the support of the child too. She spends every free minute she has with her son. The arrangement seems to suit everyone."

"You're wrong," Damon said harshly. "It doesn't suit me." His feet crashed to the floor as he sat upright and reached for the manila envelope. "You keep calling him 'the child.' I don't even know my son's name. Nothing."

"His name appears as Michael Brandel on the birth certificate," Updike said.

"The hell it does." Damon's eyes were blazing in his taut face. "Not even my name. I suppose she conceived the baby through immaculate conception."

Updike took a hurried step back. "I'm only reporting what I found."

"Then report one more bit of information. What's my son's birth date?"

"September nineteenth."

"September." Damon began to swear with soft violence. "Then she knew before— Damn her, she had to have known she was pregnant before I came back to Kasmara."

"Sheikh El Karim, I hope—" Updike stopped

and inhaled sharply as Damon's gaze shifted to his face. Rage. Hot, searing, uncontrolled fury.

Selim rose quickly to his feet. "I think you'd better go now, Updike. I'll walk you to the helicopter and tell the guards you have permission to leave."

Permission to leave, Updike thought in disgust. He always felt as if he had been hurled back into another century when he came to Kasmara. At times the imperious world of power in which the sheikh lived even struck him as funny. Yet at the moment he felt no amusement at being here. There was too much anger, too much intensity and leashed violence building in the man sitting at the desk. "I do have to get back to New York. Do you have any instructions for me?"

"No." Damon tore open the envelope. "Leave the videotape on."

Updike hastily placed the control on the desk before standing there hesitation. "The bonus?"

"You'll get your bonus." Damon spread the photographs on the desk. "Give him a check, Selim."

Selim nodded as he crossed the room and opened the door. "I'll express it to you later today." He gestured toward the open door.

"Good-bye, Sheikh El Karim." Updike hurried toward the door. "If there's anything I can do . . ."

Damon didn't answer, his gaze focused with total absorption on the pictures before him.

He was still staring at the pictures fifteen minutes later when Selim came back into the study and crossed the room to drop down onto the visitor's chair again. "There's no mistake?" Selim asked gently. "The child is definitely yours?"

"The child is mine." Damon didn't look up. "You saw the resemblance even before I did."

"I grew up with you." Selim smiled faintly. "For a minute I thought I was seeing a picture of you as a child. Still, it could have been coincidence."

"No coincidence. The child was conceived four years ago when I went to New York to sign the papers for the purchase of United Trust."

"And stayed four months after that business was finished," Selim added. "I wondered why you didn't return at once. You usually can't wait to get back to Kasmara. It was the woman?"

"No," Damon said violently. "Do you think any woman could keep me tied to her, at her beck and call, for that long? I found her good in bed but there was nothing special enough about her to keep me there." His hands tightened on the photographs. "Nothing at all."

"Really?" Selim leaned back in his chair and stretched his long legs out before him. "As I recall, when you came back to Kasmara you were like a scorpion, stinging everyone around you for at least six months. I wondered at the time—"

"It's not your place to wonder," Damon cut through his words, his face clouding stormily. "You have no right to—" He stopped. Selim was laughing, his dark eyes alight with mischief.

Selim made a mocking obeisance. "Yes, O Master. I forgot for a moment my lowly position on this earth. Are you going to send me back to my tribe with word that I've displeased you?"

Damon scowled. "I was thinking more of something on the order of my pitching you into the fountain in the courtyard. And you have your own sting, damn you."

Selim sobered. "I didn't mean to sting you." He felt a stirring of remorse. Damon always retreated behind the wall of royal arrogance when he felt threatened or was raw and hurting. Selim knew him too well to miss the defensive emotional maneuver now. "What can I do to help?"

"Nothing." Damon's shoulders were rigid with strain. "There's nothing anyone can do." His hands slowly clenched into fists. "Three years. He was mine and she cheated me out of three years of his life. She didn't tell me."

"Maybe she thought you wouldn't be interested. Men are more casual about these things."

"Casual?" Damon's fist crashed down on the desk. "Would I be casual about my son?"

Selim knew very well that Damon would react with passionate possession toward anything or anyone he felt belonged to him. "You said the relationship wasn't important. It's possible she didn't realize—"

"She realized," Damon said harshly. "She's a very intelligent woman and she knew how I'd feel and still she—" He broke off. "I want to *strangle* her."

"That's what you'd like to do," Selim said quietly. "Now, what are you going to do?"

"Probably strangle her."

"Damon . . ." Selim shook his head. He had never seen Damon this enraged. There was no use trying to reason with him until he calmed down. If he ever did calm down, Selim added ruefully to himself. "Let me rephrase it. What are you going to do immediately?"

"Go get my son."

"That goes without saying. I was mentally packing your bags from the minute I saw the picture of the boy. He's an American citizen. There may be problems."

"He's also a citizen of Sedikhan and heir to the Sheikhdom of El Zabor." Damon smiled tigerishly. "And possession has always been nine tenths of the law."

"His mother—"

"His mother gave my son to strangers to raise," he said fiercely. "Do you think I should consider her feelings? She *cheated* me. And by heaven, I'll find a way to punish her for it."

Selim stood up. "Then I assume you'll want me to make travel arrangements. When do you want to leave?"

"As soon as possible," Damon said curtly. "And try to contact Updike before he boards his flight at Marasef. I want him to travel back to New York on the Learjet with me."

Selim looked at him in surprise. "Why? I thought you were through with him."

"I wasn't thinking, I was feeling," Damon said.

"I'll need to know more about the Langstroms."
He gestured impatiently. "And . . . oh, everything.
Just get him."

Selim nodded as he strode toward the door.
"Right away. I'll have your bags packed and the
Learjet readied. I'll call you when the helicopter
returns from Marasef." The door closed behind
him.

Damon looked up from the photographs and
gazed blindly at the Rubens painting on the wall
across the room.

A son. Dear Lord, he had a son.

Now that the first stunning surprise was gone,
he was filled with a tumult of emotions. Protectiveness, curiosity, possessiveness. A child he could
love. A child who could love him. Love to fill the
loneliness he had always known. Pain suddenly
wrenched through him. But would his son love
him? Had Cory poisoned the boy against him?
Did his son believe his father had deserted him?

Anger tore through him, burning away the pain.
Cory had no right to keep his son from him. He
drew a deep breath and tried to cool his temper.
He couldn't think when he was angry, and he had
to make plans. He would have his son and he
would punish Cory. There was no question in his
mind that both things would come to pass, but
he must determine how.

He reached out, picked up the remote control,
and punched the rewind button and then play.
Cory's laughing face soon appeared on the screen

and he felt a queer jolt deep within him. Anger, he told himself. It had to be anger. She was nothing to him. Not any longer.

She hadn't meant anything to him then either. Not really. She had been just a woman to slake his lust. But she hadn't slaked it. His desire for her had been a thirst that had become unquenchable.

He'd had many women since who were more expert in pleasing a man. What was there about Cory that had caught his imagination as well as his body?

What did it matter, he wondered impatiently. He thirsted now only for revenge. No, that wasn't quite true. The anger was there but his body was even now stirring, readying itself as he remembered the feel of her, the scent of her, the way she moved beneath him.

His thumb punched down on the off button of the remote control and Cory disappeared from the screen.

He wouldn't *have* it, dammit. He wouldn't be held captive by Cory Brandel again. She was nothing to him.

Only a thirst . . .

"For heaven's sake, Cory, it's almost four o'clock in the morning. Let me call you a taxi." Gary Koenig frowned in concern. "With my luck you'll get mugged or raped on the way to the station and then I really will cut my throat."

Cory shook her head. "I feel like walking. The train station is only a few blocks away and I need the fresh air." She wrinkled her nose. "So does this apartment. Don't you ever open the windows?"

"I never think about it." Gary rubbed his stubbled jaw. "I need a shave."

"And a shower. Your suit will be ready at the cleaners in the morning. Remember to pick it up."

"I will." He opened the door and leaned wearily against the jamb. "Thanks for staying, Cory."

"No big deal." A glowing smile lit her face. "What are friends for?"

"It *was* a big deal. I don't think I would have made it this time."

"Sure you would." Cory fastened the belt of her trench coat. "Just as you'll make it the next time and the time after that. I'm just hanging around to give positive reenforcement. I'm glad I could help." She started to close the door.

"Cory?"

She stopped and looked at him inquiringly.

"Be careful." He smiled with an effort. "There aren't many people like you around. We can't afford to lose you."

She waved casually, closed the door, and began to walk down the hall toward the stairs. Her bright smile faded and then vanished entirely as the weariness she had held at bay swept over her. It was stupid to let these hours with Gary sap her strength like this. Usually she could work around the clock and still have energy to spare. She had always believed that you were tired only if you let yourself be tired. Determination and strength of will weren't the best substitute for rest, but they'd keep her going.

No, it wasn't the physical but the emotional burdens Gary hung on her that she had problems coping with. Sometimes Gary's depressions almost overwhelmed her and she was tempted to forget everything and everyone and run away to a place where she had only Michael and herself to worry about. Lord, how she'd wanted to go home to Michael when she'd left the network last night.

But you couldn't run away from friends when they needed you. Their burdens became your burdens too.

She stepped out of the apartment building onto the sidewalk and breathed deeply. The cool wet breeze felt like heaven after the hours in Gary's stuffy apartment. She immediately felt her spirits rise as she strolled along the rain-washed streets toward the station.

She had liked this time of morning since the days when she was a fledgling TV reporter assigned to the graveyard shift. The streets were quiet, and violence and brutality seemed far away. She knew very well that the quiet was deceptive, still, one had to take what one could get in New York.

But she didn't have to worry about New York, her job, or even Gary for the next few days. They could all coast along without Cory Brandel's help for a while. She would get on that train to Meadowpark and in a little over an hour she would be walking into the house on Brookwood Lane.

Her steps unconsciously quickened as her stride took on its customary springy bounce. She didn't have time to be tired right now.

In a little over an hour she would be with Michael.

Two

There was something *wrong*!

Cory closed the front door and stood there in the darkness, poised, taut, every sense straining. She had learned to trust her instincts and those instincts were now screaming. Yet, what could be wrong? The porch light had been left on as usual and the house was quiet. Too quiet. It was like that time in Nicaragua when the *contras*—

"Come in and join me, Cory."

She whirled toward the arched doorway leading to the shadowed living room. It couldn't be, she thought in sudden panic. Damon couldn't be here. She hadn't heard that deep, mocking voice in almost four years. She had told herself she would probably never hear it again. She had felt so safe.

The lamp flicked on to reveal Damon sprawled lazily in Carter's big leather easy chair by the picture window. His tall, muscular body was garbed in an elegant dark blue business suit that was sleekly civilized; it was completely at odds with the power he exuded that was purely physical. But then, Damon *was* physical, she thought. Physical, highly sexed, and the most passionate man she had ever encountered.

"You're surprised to see me?" Damon rose to his feet with the lithe grace she had told herself she had forgotten. She hadn't forgotten. She hadn't forgotten the crisp darkness of his hair that curled as stubbornly as Michael's, nor the glittering green of his eyes, nor the way he stood with his legs slightly astride as if challenging the world. She had buried it but hadn't forgotten any of it. Dear heaven, how she wished she had.

"You're not answering." Damon's lips twisted. "I don't believe I've ever seen you at a loss for words before. You've always known exactly what you wanted and where you were going."

Cory drew a deep, shaky breath. "Naturally, I didn't expect to see you here. Did Bettina and Carter give you permission to wait here until I came home?"

"Oh, yes, they were very cooperative." He continued silkily. "What charming friends you have. They said they'd known you for over five years, but I don't recall being introduced to them. Ah, you never did want me to meet any of your friends, though, did you?"

"It wasn't that kind of a relationship." She moistened her lips with her tongue. "I never met any of your friends either."

"I had no friends in New York."

"Oh, for heaven's sake, stop trying to give me a guilt trip," she said with sudden impatience. "You know that neither of us was interested in anything but—" She stopped and felt her heart start to pound faster as she met his narrowed gaze.

"Bed?" he suggested softly. "Or, more precisely, what we did in bed, and on the floor, and on the chairs, and on every possible surface in that suite at the Plaza. We couldn't get enough, could we?" His expression hardened. "Or should I say I couldn't get enough? You're the one who decided you were bored and called it quits. You didn't even bother to tell me to my face. Just a note delivered by messenger and then you were off to Rome to cover a story."

"I've never liked to drag out good-byes." She forced a smile. "And I noticed you never tried to contact me, so you must have felt the same way."

"Of course I did." He lifted his chin with royal disdain. "You were nothing more to me than I was to you. Less."

Cory experienced an odd sharp pain. "Then I obviously did the right thing. A relationship based purely on sex has a tendency to become obsessive, and I'm sure neither of us wanted that."

"No, of course we didn't." His black brows suddenly knotted in a fierce frown. "But you didn't do the right thing in not telling me about my son, damn you."

She went still. It shouldn't have come as such a shock. Why else would Damon be here? "You know about Michael?"

"Yes." The word was bitten out with barely controlled fury. "Oh, yes, Cory, I know now that you bore me a son. I know now that you cheated me out of three years of his life, and that you would have cheated me out of all the years I might have had with him if you'd had your way."

"He's *my* son," she said fiercely. "I gave birth to him; I raised him."

"You gave him to your friends to raise. What kind of mother does that make you?"

"A damn good mother. Bettina loves Michael as much as she does her own little girl. I have a career that demands I spend time out of the country. Should I have put Michael in a nursery?"

"You should have given him to me to raise." Damon's eyes were glittering. "He's my son."

She shook her head. "No way. If there was one thing I learned about you four years ago, it was that you steam-rollered over everyone around you. I'm not about to have Michael flattened by you."

"I never rolled over you."

She laughed incredulously. "You never let me have a say in anything. Whenever you wanted me, you had me. It was like being swept away by a tornado. I had no will of my own. Why do you think I tipped my hat and flitted off to Rome when I found out I was pregnant? I wasn't about to let you rob me of my child any more than I let you rob me of my independence."

"So you decided to rob me instead?" Damon's voice had lowered to a tone of soft menace. "Why did you think I'd let you do that?"

"You weren't supposed to know about Michael. How could you be robbed of something you didn't know existed?"

"So simple." Damon's lips twisted. "But life isn't so simple and neither are the consequences of deception, Cory."

"You can't have Michael," she said fiercely. "If you try to take him, I'll fight you all the way to the Supreme Court."

"Who said I'd go through the courts? Does that sound like something I'd do, Cory?"

No, the courts would be too slow for Damon, Cory thought with rising panic. Too slow and too tame for a man who was totally untamed. "Then what do you intend to do?"

"It's already done."

Cory tensed. "Are you trying to frighten me?"

He shook his head. "Michael is on his way to Sedikhan."

"No! You're lying. You have to be—" She turned and tore from the room, taking the steps two at a time to the second floor. She threw open the door to Michael's room and switched on the overhead light.

Michael's bed was empty, his covers thrown helter-skelter, the closet door ajar. She stood there staring at the empty bed while terror turned her sick with cold.

"He's quite safe." Damon said from behind her.

"And very excited to meet his father." He paused, and when he spoke again, there was a hint of huskiness in his voice. "Almost as excited as I was to meet my son. *Damn* you for keeping us apart, Cory."

She whirled to face him. "He belongs to me. You can't do this. It's kidnapping, Damon. There are laws in this country."

"So I've heard. But I'm the law in Kasmara, and that's where Michael will be living from now on."

"You can't . . ." Her hands clenched helplessly into fists at her sides. "He's only a little boy. You can't take him from everything that's familiar, everyone he knows and loves."

"But I'm not," Damon said calmly. "Of course, the surroundings will be new, but I'm making sure there will be a familiar anchor for him to cling to until he becomes accustomed to me. Your friends that you place so much confidence in accompanied him."

"Carter and Bettina?" She shook her head dazedly. "You kidnapped them too? This is getting wilder by the minute."

"Not kidnapped." Damon smiled faintly. "I merely offered Carter a very lucrative position as manager of my new power plant in Kasmara. I stressed how urgent it was he take over the job at once and that naturally you wanted such good friends to be nearby when you took your place at my side. He seemed very grateful that our differences had been resolved and everything was working out so nicely. He's a proud man and he didn't like to have to accept money from you to keep the household going."

Cory knew Dave had chafed at accepting help, but she hadn't realized that because of his pride, he would blind himself to the truth. "You lied to him."

"As you lied to me."

"I never lied to you."

"Silence can be deceptive too."

"Bettina . . ." She was wildly grasping at straws. "Bettina wouldn't have let you take Michael without first checking with me."

"You're right. She tried to call you both at the network and at home, but you couldn't be reached last night. I assume you were with Koenig?" She nodded numbly and a savage expression crossed Damon's face before he could subdue it. "How fortunate for me."

"I can't believe she'd let you take him."

"Perhaps her action was colored by the fact that she was very grateful her husband was going to be his own man again. And then, too, a kidnapper doesn't usually abduct an entire household."

"Only if he's Damon El Karim," she said bitterly.

He bowed slightly. "True. They didn't realize what a barbarian I am." He paused. "Any more than you do."

"I realize," she said grimly. Her nails bit into her palms as her hands clenched tighter. "You can't get away with it, Damon. I'll get Michael back from you."

"Sedikhan is a monarchy and Alex Ben Raschid

has refused to sign any extradition treaties." He paused. "And since Alex and I are cousins, I somehow doubt if he could be coerced by your government."

She felt a surge of wild despair.. "I'd like to strangle you."

"How very barbaric of you, Cory. Are we reversing roles now?" The mockery in his face was suddenly replaced by grimness. "However, I must admit that's exactly how I felt about you when I found out about Michael. The only thing that kept me going was the thought I'd soon be able to punish you for keeping my son from me."

"By victimizing a little boy?"

"Michael won't be victimized. Do you think I'd hurt my own son?" He shook his head. "Oh, no, it's you I want to punish. I thought long and hard on the plane trip here how I was going to go about that. Do you know what I decided?"

"Splinters beneath my nails?" she asked flippantly. "I wouldn't put it past you."

"Then perhaps you know me better than I thought you did. The idea has a certain appeal." He shook his head. "But I think I've found a way to hurt you more. Something that will hurt you unbearably because it will strike at the independence you hold so dear. I've decided to make you my *kiran*."

"You won't make me anything. I'm the one who decides what I'll do or not do."

"Aren't you even going to ask what a *kiran* is?" Damon asked mockingly. "I'll tell you anyway. In my country there are three types of women of pleasure. The prostitute who gives herself to all who can pay. The *kadin*, who is also for sale but is respected much as the Japanese geisha, and the *kiran*, who falls somewhere between them. A *kiran* belongs to only one man and gives pleasure anytime, anywhere, and in any way her master decrees. Her body, her conversation, her mind are always at his disposal."

"Master?" Cory asked in disbelief. "You're talking about sexual slavery? That sort of thing doesn't even exist anymore."

"It doesn't in Kasmara any longer. I published an edict banning unwilling servitude of any nature." He smiled. "But I've decided to make an exception in your case."

He meant it, she realized incredulously. He meant every word he had said. His anger and bitterness radiated across the room to envelop her in searing bands of emotion. "You're crazy. I'd never let myself be used like that."

"I think you will. Think of the alternatives. You can stay here and bloody your fists trying to beat through the walls of diplomatic red tape to try to get Michael back. You may even succeed in twenty or thirty years. Or you can come to Kasmara as my *kiran*. If you please me, I may even give you a house nearby where you can visit with Michael." He nodded as he saw the flare of rage in her eyes. "I take it the idea doesn't please you. Yet I'm at least giving you the opportunity to see your son. You didn't give me the same option."

"You arrogant bastard."

"Yes, I am. But that's beside the point. There's one more thing you might consider. If you come to Kasmara, you might have the opportunity of spiriting Michael away and out of Sedikhan. I'd think that aspect would appeal to you."

It *did* appeal to her. It was the only light of hope in this entire nightmare Damon had spun.

"I can see that it does." Damon's gaze was searching her face. "It's only fair to tell you the chances are extremely slim of such a thing happening. My people are loyal to me and I have no intentions of permitting you to leave until I'm ready. Once there, you'll be as much a prisoner as I—" He broke off and shrugged. "I thought you should know."

She felt an instant of surprise at his honesty. He'd had no need to spell out the pitfalls when he held all the cards. Then surprise was submerged once again by anger. "How kind of you to warn me," she said caustically. "Or did you want only to make me feel more helpless?"

"I do want you to feel helpless, but there are more pleasant ways to accomplish that." His gaze moved over her lingeringly. "Perhaps you remember a few of them."

Cory experienced a sudden mindless surge of heat stirring within her as memories she had suppressed came tumbling to the forefront. Dear heaven, no, she thought desperately. What she was feeling couldn't be desire. That had ended a long time ago. "I don't remember anything."

"You do." His gaze was on her face. "You wouldn't

let me possess any other part of you, but you did give me your body. Totally. Completely. As I gave mine to you."

"You never gave me anything. I was the one who was subjugated. I was no more to you than one of those stupid *kirans*."

"That's not the way I remember it." Damon made an impatient gesture. "No matter. If you think I treated you as a *kiran*, perhaps it's just as well that you'll now have the title. You may even learn to enjoy the role. You still want me."

"I *don't* want you. I think I may even hate you."

"Your mind may hate me but that doesn't prevent your body from sending out signals to you." He smiled. "And to me. There's been too much between us not to have developed certain automatic responses." His gaze went to her breasts outlined against the tan trench coat. "I wonder what I'd find if I took off that trench coat and whatever you're wearing beneath it? Are your breasts swelling, Cory? Are your nipples becoming hard and poi— "

"No!" Her hand went defensively to the throat of her trench coat and she took a hurried step back. She knew color was staining her cheeks and she hated that betrayal as much as the other hidden one he had guessed was taking place. As much as she hated him.

Yet, if she hated him, why couldn't she cut off this damnable physical response? She had always been a rational, thinking human being.

Except where Damon was concerned.

Her reaction to him had never even approached rationality until she had managed to gather her strength to leave him. And only the shock of finding she was pregnant had enabled her to do so. "That was a long time ago. I don't feel anything for you now."

"I think you're lying." Damon's eyes were suddenly blazing. "But I'm not afraid to tell the truth. I still want you. I'm looking at you and all I want is to take off your clothes and come into you." His lips twisted. "I'm ready right now. You remember how I could never wait to have you. The minute you unlocked the door and came into the suite I'd rush you into the bedroom."

Sometimes he hadn't even waited to get to the bedroom, she recalled with a hot shiver. They'd made love on the floor of the foyer or the couch in the sitting room—

"You once told me you thought about coming back to me all day as you went about your job, knowing what was waiting for you as you walked through the door. You were always ready. Always as wild as I was."

She took a deep breath. "Maybe I was wild as you then, but I've grown up a little and look for more than sex in my relationships now."

"It *was* more than sex. It was—" He stopped and was silent a moment before shrugging his shoulders. "It was obsession."

"It could have become an obsession. That's why I put an end to it."

"*Your* decision. *Your* choice. *Your* child. None

of it mine," he said harshly. "I think it's time I took an active part in this relationship."

"There is no relationship."

"You're the mother of my child. That constitutes a fairly intimate bond among the El Zabor, if not in this society."

"I don't know anything about the El Zabor, but I can—"

"You'll learn," he interrupted. "You'll learn all about me. No one knows a man like his *kiran*." His smile was suddenly bittersweet. "You were never interested before in anything but the pleasure I gave you. Perhaps you'll find it to your advantage to study me more closely this time."

He was determined to go through with this madness, she realized in hopeless despair. She had to try to reason with him one more time. "Damon, maybe I should have told you about Michael, but you have to admit there was no mention of commitment in our relationship. How would I know you'd even want a child?"

"You knew."

Yes, she had known, Cory thought. She had known how possessive Damon could be and how he would react at the possibility of a son. He would have swept him away from her at birth just as he was doing now. "He's my son, Damon," she whispered. "I love him. Give him back to me."

A multitude of emotions crossed Damon's face as he gazed at her. "I know you love him. I saw your face . . ." He shook his head as if to clear it. "You didn't give me a chance to love him, even to get to know him. I'm taking that chance now. Michael stays in Kasmara and, if you want to go to Kasmara to be with him, it will be only on my terms."

"*Kiran*, Cory said bitterly.

He nodded. "*Kiran.*"

She stood there looking at him, anger and frustration flooding through her in a hot tide. "I'll never forgive you for this."

"I don't ask for forgiveness. What's your decision?"

"There is no decision. What else can I do?" Her voice was trembling with anger. "But you listen to me, Damon. I'll be your little toy, I'll do whatever you say. But it won't last long. I'm going to take my son away from you, and when I do, I'll make sure you can never do this again. Do you understand?"

To her surprise there was no anger in his expression, only respect and admiration. "It's what I expected of you. I wouldn't have it any other way." He glanced at his watch. "I sent Michael and the Langstroms to Sedikhan in my jet, so I've chartered another plane to leave from a private airport on Long Island. I told them I'd be ready to leave at ten. That should give you plenty of time to call the network and tell them you're going away."

"You know, of course, that going off like this may do serious damage to my career. They may even tell me never to come back."

"You're far too valuable for them to write you off," Damon said. "And you should have thought of that when you decided to rob me of my son."

"Rob? I didn't rob—" She stopped and whirled on her heel. "You may have to postpone your plans. I have to make other calls if I'm going to be away for a while."

"Koenig?" Damon's voice chopped like a machete.

"Among other people." She frowned. "You mentioned Gary before. How did you know that I—"

"That doesn't matter," he broke in impatiently with an imperious wave of his hand. "Go ahead and make your calls. I'll wait."

"Thank you." Her tone dripped irony. "I would have done it anyway."

"I'll allow you your independence." He paused before continuing silkily. "But only until you board the plane. After that you become *kiran*. And make no mistake, Cory, the minute you forget to play the role is the minute I'll have you escorted over the Sedikhan border." He added softly, "without Michael."

She could feel the muscles along her spine tense and ripple with instinctive rejection like a cat arching with anger or fear. That must not happen. Under no circumstances must she be separated from Michael until she could get them both out of Sedikhan. "I understand." She glanced defiantly over her shoulder. "You said I don't know you, Damon. Well, you don't know me either. I have the strength to play your erotic fantasy games and still stay my own person. I've fought a hell of a lot tougher battles than this."

"Have you?" His expression became arrested. "I wonder what battles you're talking about. You're right, I don't really know you. You never let me get close enough. Perhaps there will be some interesting revelations for both of us."

"Not for me. I don't want to know you, Damon."

His smile held an odd sadness. "You never did." He turned away. "Go make your calls. I had Bettina Langstrom pack a bag for you before they left. I didn't think you'd want one of my men handling your possessions."

Again surprise poured through her, dissipating a minute portion of her resentment. How could Damon be so exquisitely sensitive to a woman's feelings of violation and still be so ruthlessly demanding? "I'll need more than one bag if you're going to insist on this insanity."

He shook his head, and the expression on his face was suddenly blatantly sensual. "As my *kiran* it will be my pleasure to dress you." He smiled with an intimacy that caused her to catch her breath. "And undress you."

Heat rippled through her, and she felt the muscles of her stomach clench with a response as familiar as it was intense. No, she mustn't want him. It was insane to want an enemy, to hunger for his touch. . . . She mustn't give him more than acquiescence. She turned her face away and started again down the corridor. "I'll be down when I've made my arrangements and not before."

"Take all the time you like. Do anything you like." He added softly from behind her, "Until you board that plane."

Her pace quickened until it held an element of

flight as she hurried down the corridor to her room.

The two brawny young men standing on either side of the door of the plane were dressed in well-tailored business suits but their vigilance betrayed their occupation. Cory had seen their like hovering over power figures in every corner of the world.

The taller of the two bowed to Damon. "All is well, *Bardono*?"

"All is well." Damon's hand tightened on Cory's arm. "Cory, these gentlemen are Abdul and Hassan. You'll be seeing them frequently."

"Bodyguards," she said tersely. "Considering what an arrogant bastard you are, I'd say you probably need them. You must manage to antagonize everyone you meet."

A stunned expression appeared on Abdul's face before he took a threatening step forward. "*Bardono*, disrespect . . ."

Damon lifted his hand and said quietly, "It is permitted. The woman is mine."

"Bull," Cory said succinctly.

Abdul looked uncertainly at Damon before he stepped back again. "If it is your wish." He glared at Cory. "But it is disrespect."

The smaller guard Damon had introduced as Hassan said quickly, "The pilot is ready to take off at your word, *Bardono*."

"Then give the word." Damon urged Cory up

the steps. "And once we're airborne, I don't wish to be disturbed until I summon you."

Hassan bowed.

"I can't believe this," Cory muttered as she entered the passenger compartment. "No wonder you're so impossible, with all that fawning over you. I don't remember you being surrounded by bodyguards before."

"They were there. I just made sure they made themselves unobtrusive." He propelled her down the lushly carpeted aisle toward two black velvet upholstered executive chairs in the rear of the plane. "You were already wary of me as it was. I was too wild for you, my culture too different. Do you think I couldn't see that? So Hassan and Abdul stayed very much in the background."

She had been wary of him but she hadn't realized he had been conscious of her reservations. "A man who needs bodyguards obviously isn't the most desirable of companions."

"I don't *need* them but it's the custom for the sheikh of the El Zabor to be under protection at all times." He shrugged. "It doesn't matter, so I let my chieftains have their way."

The engines of the jet began to rev and Cory felt a sudden flutter of panic. She cast a wild glance at Damon and found his gaze on her face as if he had been expecting her reaction. "It's not too late. You can get off the plane. Your choice."

"Without Michael."

He nodded. "It's my turn, Cory."

She swallowed and glanced away. She quickly

undid the belt of her trench coat and slipped it off. "The hell it is." She slung her coat on the glass coffee table in front of the chairs. "I'm going to Kasmara." She dropped onto the window seat and began to fasten her seat belt. "And I'm going to make you sorry every minute I'm there."

For a moment relief conflicted with a strange sadness in his expression. "I imagine we'll both have enough cause for regret before this is over. I'm going to the cockpit, but I'll be back one we're airborne."

"Stay as long as you like. You won't be missed."

"I know." He smiled crookedly. You haven't missed me for the last four years. Why should this be any different?" He strode down the aisle toward the cockpit without giving her a chance to reply.

He was wrong. She had missed him at first, before time had managed to reinforce the barriers she had locked in place to keep the memory of him at bay. She would wake in the middle of the night, her body throbbing, needing him with a hunger that was as fierce as it was mindless. She imagined his face above her, intense and sensual. She had been able almost to feel his hands on her flesh.

She drew a deep quivering breath and turned her head to gaze blindly out the window. She wouldn't think about the period of madness they'd shared. It was gone. She had known at the time that Damon was wrong for her and she'd never be able to tolerate a man so dominating, so demanding.

She had accepted him into her bed because she

hadn't been able to resist the strength of the sexual attraction whirling them both away, but she had protected herself from any deeper involvement. Just as she would protect herself again now that he had come back into her life.

"It will be a long flight."

She stiffened as her gaze flew to Damon standing in the aisle with a folded red blanket in his hands. They were airborne. She hadn't realized so much time had passed. "How long?"

"We'll be landing in Marasef tomorrow morning and change to a helicopter to take us to Kasmara." He sat down beside her and spread the blanket over both of them. "We'll arrive there before sundown."

She started to push the blanket aside. "I don't need this. I'm not cold."

"You'll need it." Damon pulled the blanket up around her shoulders. *"Kiran."*

Her eyes widened in surprise.

He smiled crookedly. "Did you forget? I assure you I didn't. We're en route to Kasmara, Cory, and that means our agreement is in full force." His voice thickened. "I want to touch you."

Her gaze flew to the guards sitting in the front of the plane. Her lungs seemed suddenly robbed of air. "Here?"

"When did we ever require a conventional setting? The blanket is only to make you feel more secure. Abdul and Hassan won't disturb us by so much as a glance." He paused. "Unbutton your blouse."

"No I—" She met his gaze and stopped, held by the sheer force of his will.

"Do it," he said softly. *"Kiran."*

Her hands moved slowly to the buttons on the front of her blouse. She was trembling, she realized, but there was no chill, only heat. Every shivering breath she drew seared through her as if she were inhaling fire.

"Are they unbuttoned?"

"Yes."

"And now the bra. I remember those pretty lacy cups and how they framed your breasts. You always wore bras that fastened in front. Do you still?"

She nodded jerkily.

"Then get rid of it and the blouse too."

"Damon, this isn't . . ." She met his gaze and almost instinctively her hands moved to do as he commanded.

The bra and the blouse fluttered to the floor.

"Now the rest of your clothes."

Her hands moved with dreamlike slowness beneath the blanket, conscious only of tingling heat and Damon's gaze fixed intently on her face. Then it was done and she leaned back in the chair, the plushness of the material soft and furlike on her bare flesh.

Damon wasn't touching her, but the furnacelike heat of his body enveloped her beneath the blanket. She could feel her body respond helplessly to the knowledge that she was sitting naked, in compliance with his wishes. "I don't like this, Damon."

"Yes, you do." He smiled down at her. "This isn't too different from other fantasies we've acted out in the past."

"But this is real."

"And so you're finding it even more exciting. I may not know your mind, but I do know your body, Cory. You're sitting there waiting for me to touch you, every muscle tense and tingling. Your breasts are swelling and you want me."

"You don't know that. You can't see . . ." She moistened her lips with her tongue. "It's your imagination."

"No, it's *your* imagination. You have such a splendid imagination, Cory. You're imagining how it's going to feel to have my hands on you again; you're visualizing what I'm going to do to you."

He was right, she realized. Her mind was a tumult of pictures, memories, and anticipations melting together in a wild stream.

"But it's not going to happen yet." He settled back in his chair. "We're just going to sit here for a while. I'm not going to touch you. Not even with one finger. You won't know when or how the first touch will come."

He wanted her. She could see that the muscles of his shoulders were tense and rigid and his voice was hoarse. Yet, if he said he would wait, he would wait. His control had often astounded her. "Is that part of my punishment?"

"If it is, then I'm punishing myself too." A muscle jumped in his cheek. "It's torture."

But he wouldn't break until he was ready. She

tried to relax, but it was impossible. She sat there, waiting. The plush velvet caressing her skin, Damon's gaze on her face, her heart pounding so hard she thought it would jump from her breast.

The first touch came fifteen minutes later. Damon's fingertips lightly grazed her left breast. She gasped, her muscles convulsed. After the minutes of tension it was like an electric shock. Her gaze flew to his face.

His green eyes were glittering as his warm palm slowly cupped her breast. "Do you know how many times in the last four years I've awakened in the night to find myself reaching out, searching for you?" His hand compressed, squeezed gently. "Thinking how the weight of you felt in my hand." His thumbnail lightly flicked her nipple and she inhaled sharply. "How you'd harden and swell. How I'd love to make you gasp as you did just now. Did you think about that too?" He smiled crookedly. "No, I guess not. But you're thinking now, aren't you, Cory?"

She could think of nothing else as his hands roamed over her body. Exploring, playing, toying, stroking until she thought she'd go up in flames. Her teeth bit into her lower lip to keep back the moan that trembled in her throat.

"No, don't make a sound." Damon's eyes were blazing down at her, his nostrils flaring. "I don't want anyone to hear the little cries you make when I'm loving you. They're mine, just as you're mine."

"No, I'm not—" She broke off as his hands clasped her breasts. Heat. Shock. Hunger.

"You *are* mine. Always." His voice held an intensity that shocked her. "You were mine then and you're mine now."

She fought her way through the field of sensuality he was spinning around her. "It's not true. I'll never be what you want me to be."

"You don't even know what I want you to be," he said roughly. "You weren't interested enough to ask."

"This is what you want me to be," she cried. "Your damn *kiran*. That's what you always wanted."

"That's not what I wanted then. I wanted—" He broke off and was silent, his chest moving harshly with the force of his breathing. "I wanted many things in addition to this."

"But sex is what you took."

"Sex is what you gave," he said fiercely. "I didn't take then and I'm not taking now."

"How can you say that?" she asked incredulously.

"Perhaps I'm forcing you into a certain position, but you're responding." He frowned moodily. "Your body doesn't lie."

She drew a shaky breath. "I'm a normal woman with needs you're capable of arousing. But that's all, Damon."

She saw the pain in his eyes. "Then that will have to be enough, won't it?"

She turned her head to look out the window. "May I put my clothes on now?"

He was silent a moment, and when he spoke

his tone held a note of mockery. "I think not." His hand moved beneath the red blanket, one finger trailing slowly down her body to rest between her thighs. He smiled as he felt the muscles of her stomach clench and the trembling start again. "Perhaps in a few hours. I believe we'll leave the actual consummation until we reach Kasmara." He found what he was searching for and heard Cory gasp as the pad of his fingertip pressed and then began to slowly rotate. "But, as I said, it's a long flight and a man must have some distraction."

Cory was asleep.

Damon gazed down at her and a wave of unbearable loneliness swept through him. She had gone away from him again, left him isolated and alone. He had forgotten those moments when he had watched her sleep, knowing she was no longer his, that he could hold her for only fleet moments before she once more closed him out. Even in sleep she had done it. Instead of cuddling close to him, she had always turned away, curling up in a ball in her own space, instinctively rejecting him. She was doing the same thing now, huddling against the wall of the plane, her head leaning against the window. He wanted to reach out and touch her, bring her back to him.

Why not? Things were different this time. He didn't have to worry about her leaving him; he didn't have to worry about rejection.

But he didn't wake her.

Because things weren't different.

He didn't wake her for the same reason he hadn't done it all those many times in the past. Because a bewildering river of emotion was storming through him now just as it had then. And its driving current was . . . tenderness.

Three

"This is Selim Abol, Cory. He's my executive assistant and resident financial wizard." Damon smiled wryly. "And also my conscience."

"I don't know how he's doing with the rest of his tasks, but he could do a hell of a lot better on the conscience bit," Cory said as she passed Selim without a glance and started down the hall. "Where are the slaves kept in this Taj Mahal?"

"Cory"—there was an edge to Damon's voice—"I forgot to add one other position Selim fills here. He's my good friend and my *kiran* does not treat him with discourtesy."

"*Kiran.*" There was shock in Selim's soft murmur. "Oh, Lord . . ."

Cory whirled to face him. "I suppose you have a *kiran* stashed away somewhere too? It seems to be the male prerogative in this blasted stronghold of male chauvinism." She would have gone on but paused as she met Selim's gaze. There was nothing but sympathy and apprehension in the young man's expression and her annoyance abruptly vanished. "You're not fortunate in your friends, Selim, but I don't suppose I should blame you for Damon's sins."

A sudden twinkle appeared in Selim's eyes. "I hope not. I have quite enough of my own to worry about. I'd be weighted down like the ancient mariner if you hung Damon's iniquities about my neck."

Cory's lips curved in a reluctant smile. "You'd never be able to lift your head," she agreed as she ran her fingers wearily through her hair. Heavens, her hair felt as mussed and soiled as the rest of her. "Do you suppose you could find me a bed and a bath somewhere in the midst of all this grandeur? I don't think I've slept more than a few hours in the past two days." She shot Damon a resentful glance. "I never sleep well on planes."

"I'll take the responsibility for your wakefulness for the last thirty hours or so, but you'll have to blame Koenig for the night before." There was violence beneath the silkiness in Damon's voice. "He must have been very . . . demanding."

"Oh, he was," she said sweetly. "Gary is always demanding."

Anger flared in Damon's eyes as he took an impulsive step forward. "Then it's lucky—"

Selim stepped between them. "I think we'll put you in the jade suite," he said quickly. He took

Cory's arm and gave her a gentle push down the corridor. "I think you'll find it interesting. It has a colorful history and was first occupied by Ralane, the favorite *kadin* of Damon's great-grandfather."

"Can it be suitable then for a lowly *kiran*?"

Selim's pace quickened. "I'll send Liande to draw your bath before you take your nap."

"For a few hours," Damon said curtly. "I want her in my suite for dinner at nine."

Cory shrugged. "If I wake up."

"If you don't, it will be my pleasure to wake you." Damon said mockingly. "And your pleasure too."

The hot color flooded her cheeks. "It won't be my—"

"Later." Selim's grip tightened on her arm as he almost pushed her down the hall. "Conversation can wait until you're less tired." As they rounded a corner Selim muttered, "And your thinking's a hell of a lot clearer."

"Do we have to run?" Cory asked.

Selim's pace slowed. "I thought it wise. Damon was about to explode and you were busy lighting new fuses with every word."

"He's arrogant."

"Yes."

"And domineering."

"Yes."

"And unprincipled."

"No." Selim shook his head. "His code may be different from yours, but he has stronger principles than anyone I know." He paused. "And he lives by them, which isn't always easy for a man in his position."

"I haven't noticed any qualms about kidnapping or—"

"Did he kidnap you?" Selim asked with mild curiosity.

"No," Cory said grimly. "But he kidnapped my son."

"It must have been a most unusual abduction. Michael seems as happy as the proverbial lark."

Her gaze flew to his face. "You've seen Michael? How is he? Was he tired from the trip? Did he seem—"

Selim held up his hand. "He's fine. He seemed a little tired, but that's to be expected. He was very eager and curious about everything. He chattered all the time we were getting him and the Langstroms settled. Is he always that loquacious?"

"Always." Cory's face was suddenly glowing with tenderness. "Nonstop. You just have to tune him out. I remember—" She stopped as she felt the tears rise helplessly to her eyes. "I want to *see* him. Where is he?"

Selim hesitated. "I can't tell you that, but I'll save you the trouble of ransacking the palace. Neither Michael not the Langstroms are on the palace grounds." He smiled sympathetically. "Perhaps Damon will permit you to see him soon."

"Permit?" She swallowed. "He's my son."

"He's Damon's son too," Selim said gravely. "And

you never permitted him to see Michael. I don't believe you know what that means to him."

"He would have wanted to own Michael."

"Yes, but he would have given him love too. Love without end, Cory." He inclined his head. "May I call you Cory?"

She nodded absently. *Love without end.* The phrase sparked an odd aching pang deep within her. "You can't defend what he's done in the name of love. He didn't even know Michael."

"Not in the name of love," Selim said gently. "But perhaps in the name of loneliness."

"Loneliness." Cory scoffed. "Good Lord, the man's surrounded by adulators. It was positively sickening how everyone bowed and scraped to him when we landed at Marasef and after we arrived here. Do all the sheikhs of Sedikhan command that kind of power?"

Selim shook his head. "Damon is the Sheikh of the El Zabor. His position is . . . different."

"How different?

"The El Zabor are bedouin tribes that still wander the desert. They've developed a complex culture in which the sheikh is regarded with almost superstitious worship by his followers."

"How pleasant," Cory said caustically. "That must be a real ego trip for Damon."

Selim shook his head. "Rarely pleasant. Damon pays his dues."

"Judging from this palace, he must keep a large percentage of those dues for himself."

"Kasmara is oil-rich, and Damon inherited a

huge fortune from his Tamrovian mother as well."
He gazed at her in surprise. "Didn't you know
that? I find it curious that you know so little
about Damon when you were so obviously—" He
paused before adding deliberately, "Intimate."

"Intimate wasn't exactly the way to describe our
relationship. It wasn't the usual—" She stopped
and tried again. "We didn't talk much." She saw
that Selim was trying to suppress a smile and
made a face at him. "Well, we didn't."

"No doubt you were occupied with other means
of communication."

"No doubt." Cory frowned. "But that isn't important now. What's important is that Damon
has taken my son from me and I have to get him
back. Clearly, you're a reasonable man, Selim.
Surely you can see that this is criminal?"

"Not in Kasmara."

"That's ridiculous." She blinked rapidly to banish the tears of sheer frustration that were threatening. "Are you telling me that he can do anything
he pleases?"

Selim nodded. "No one would dare dispute his
word. It would undermine our entire system of
justice."

"Justice? Do you call this justice?" she asked
huskily. "Help me, Selim. I want my son."

"I'll help you where I can." Selim looked troubled. "But I can't dispute Damon either. I, too, am
of the El Zabor."

"Who are clearly lost in some kind of time warp,"

Cory said bitterly. "I feel as if I've stepped back into the day of Saladin."

"Damon is struggling to change that, but it's not easy to fight against centuries of tradition."

"Particularly when he has the same mentality."

Selim stopped before a richly carved mahogany door and turned to face her. "You're right. Part of Damon is pure El Zabor, and he sometimes reacts impulsively and violently like a naughty child. But if you could understand the kind of pressures he faces, you might—"

"Taking Michael was not 'naughty,' it was criminal and I'll never forgive him for it."

"Then don't forgive him." Selim opened the door. "But try to understand him. He makes mistakes but—'"

"Kingsize mistakes."

He nodded. "Granted. But he's also a man who cares, Cory. I've never met anyone who cares as much as Damon."

She drew a deep breath. "I don't want to understand him. I only want my son back."

He smiled faintly. "Perhaps one could lead to the other."

"It's not likely," Cory said. "His goal is to punish me."

"He's angry and hurt, but once that passes he'll try to be fair. Justice is important to Damon. It's part of his training, it's part of what he is."

Cory grimaced. "A lawless sheikh?"

He turned to go. "No," he said softly. "The *Bardono*."

Before she could reply he was striding down the hall in the direction from which they had come.

Cory stood looking after him and was tempted to call him back and question him. *Bardono* was how Hassan and Abdul had addressed Damon, and she had assumed it was only a title indicating respect. It evidently had another significance.

She turned and entered the suite and shut the door. Questions could wait. Everything could wait until she had rested and regained some of her strength. It was clear it wasn't going to be a simple matter to get herself and Michael out of Kasmara; she would need to call upon all her reserves of wit and energy. Perhaps Selim was right and she should try to submerge her resentment and anger and consider all sides of the situation to see if she could find a way out of this cage in which Damon had locked her. Maybe there was something in what Selim said about understanding being the way to defeat Damon.

Oh, she just didn't know. She couldn't think straight. She leaned back against the door, her gaze wandering over the high-ceilinged room. For Pete's sake, she thought, this place looks like a blasted seraglio.

Rich Persian carpets patterned in jade green and delicate ivory spilled over white marble floors. Sheer white draperies looped over the wide, low bed that was covered in jade satin and heaped with white silk cushions. Two pillars of malachite supported a graceful archway that presumably led to the bathing area. The white fretwork on the floor-to-ceiling windows was carved in lacy patterns that permitted only fleeting glimpses of the hard blue sky beyond. Everything about the room was exotic, luxurious . . . and different from anything in her experience. She suddenly felt very much the stranger in a strange land.

She straightened away from the door and squared her shoulders. She had been in strange lands before and had always survived very well indeed. This was no different. All she had to do was get a little rest and she'd be fine.

Cory stopped just inside the door of Damon's suite and gazed at him in surprise. She had never seen him garbed in anything but the most elegant and conventional of Western clothes, usually business suits. Now black jeans clung to his muscular thighs and rode low on his hips before disappearing into kneehigh black boots whose soft leather was both worn and scuffed. His white cotton shirt was left open at the throat and the sleeves rolled casually to the elbow.

He turned away from the French doors as he heard her enter the room. One brow raised quizzically as he saw her expression. "What's the matter? Have I suddenly grown horns?"

"Not suddenly." She came forward, her gaze narrowed on him. "I'm sure you've always had them together with cloven hooves and a tail. You just kept them well hidden."

"Ah, yes." He smiled mockingly. "Satan incarnate."

"I was just surprised to see you dressed so casually. You always looked like an ad for Giorgio Armani. Now you look like—" She stopped, studying him.

"Rudolph Valentino in *The Sheik*?" he suggested sardonically.

She shook her head. "Maybe a Texas cowboy."

"I assure you I'm not trying to impress you with my romantic image. This is what I usually wear when I'm not—" He stopped abruptly.

"Not what?"

He met her gaze. "Trying to keep from scaring off wary New York ladies." He shrugged. "But now I don't have to worry about that, do I? Now it's your duty as a *kiran* to dress to please me." His gaze traveled from the filmy pink scarf draping her throat and floating behind her to the deep pink bandeau covering her breasts and finally to the volumnious extravagance of the matching harem pajamas. "And you do please me tonight." His gaze returned to the silky ripeness of her breasts overflowing the bandeau. "And later you'll please me even more."

Cory felt the familiar heat ignite and then begin to move through her as she gazed at him. She quickly averted her eyes. "Did you think it would annoy me to wear this silly outfit? Why should it? I'm not what I wear." She shrugged. "Besides, the maid Selim sent me left me little choice as to what I was going to wear. She pulled this out of the closet and wouldn't put it back. Liande is evidently as much a fan of yours as everyone else around here. She looked as if she'd burst into tears if I did anything to make you angry."

"Sensible woman." For a moment there was a ghost of a twinkle in Damon's eyes. "You might learn a great deal from her attitude."

"About being a doormat?" Cory shook her head. "No, thank you. I've already taken that course."

He frowned. "I never treated you as a doormat."

"I wasn't talking about you. I'd already graduated from that particular school before I met you."

"I suppose you wouldn't care to tell me who—" Then as he saw her expression become shuttered he smiled lopsidedly. "No, I didn't think so."

"It doesn't matter." Cory moved forward to stand beside him at the French doors, her gaze on the starlit brilliance of the night sky. "Selim gave me some advice earlier today."

"Selim is always giving advice. He thinks he can run the world."

"He's not the only one," she said dryly. "It must be a characteristic acquired by osmosis."

"Selim never tries to emulate me. He's strictly his own man. That's why I value him."

There was a note of absolute sincerity in Damon's voice that caused Cory to turn and study his face. "It's hard for me to believe you don't find all this hero worship gratifying."

"Then don't believe it," he said curtly. "You were going to tell me the advice Selim saw fit to give you."

"He said to try to understand you."

He laughed harshly. "It wasn't your understanding I wanted when I brought you to Kasmara."

"Then tell me why you did bring me."

"I thought I'd made myself crystal-clear on that point."

"I thought you had too." She met his gaze directly. "You're angry and you want to punish me. Is that all?"

"Isn't that enough?"

"It would be enough if you were as one-dimensional as I tried to convince myself you were four years ago. But now I'm not so sure."

"Should I be flattered that you no longer consider me as transparent?"

"I didn't say that," she said calmly. "I've just realized you may be an unknown quantity, and it's important that I not go up against an opponent I know nothing about. So I'm going to find out everything I can about you." She smiled through her teeth as she added, "So I can take my son away from you and make sure you never get near him again."

"Sweet understanding," Damon said ironically.

"I don't feel sweet toward you, Damon. I feel bewildered and mad as hell."

"And you want me."

She met his gaze fearlessly. "Yes, I want you. I won't lie to you. I'd be stupid to try when we both know what you did to me on the plane. Now it's time for you to tell me the truth. What else do you feel for me?"

"So that you can use it against me?"

She nodded. "So that I can use it against you."

"You must think I'm an idiot to—" He stopped and gazed at her broodingly for a long moment before he said grudgingly, "Hell, maybe I am an idiot. What are you to me? You're a raging thirst. You always were. I could never get enough of you."

"So you didn't get your fill of me in your bed four years ago and thought you'd continue our affair on your own terms. Is that correct?"

"Damn, you're cool." Damon turned on his heel, strode across the room, and jabbed at the inter-com button on the sofa table. "I feel as if I'm on the witness stand being cross-examined."

"I'm not cool." There was the slightest quaver in her voice. "This isn't easy for me. I want to scream and beat my fists on the wall and do all the stupid, childish things that would make me feel better and accomplish absolutely nothing. Instead, I have to try to understand what makes you tick. I have to think logically and analytically." She drew a deep breath. "And I'll do it, dammit."

"I think you will," he said slowly. "I never realized you were this—"

"Aggressive?" She finished for him. "I have a moderate amount of aggressiveness. Every career woman has to be assertive these days or she ends up at the short end."

"That isn't the word I would have chosen."

"I'm almost afraid to ask what word you did have in mind."

"Strength," he said softly. "I thought it was only

stubbornness and determination, but it's strength."
His eyes were intent as they searched her face.
"Perhaps I didn't want to recognize it as strength."

"Then maybe you need to understand me as
much as I need to understand you." She raised
her chin with a touch of defiance. "Shall we call a
truce?"

"To probe each other's weaknesses?"

"And evaluate each other's strengths."

He stood looking at her for a moment, and she
thought he was going to refuse. Then he gave her
a smile of surprising sweetness. "Why not? It might
be interesting to discover if you can see me as I
am without running for cover."

The door opened and a damask-covered table
was wheeled into the room by two white-coated
servants who bowed obsequiously to Damon.

He motioned toward the French doors and
snapped his fingers. The table was immediately
wheeled to the place he'd indicated, and the two
servants began to tidy up the table settings.

"Do you always snap your fingers when you
want service?" Cory asked.

"Did I do that?" He made a face and suddenly
looked like a little boy caught in mischief. "It's the
custom, but I've been trying to break myself of the
habit. It was pointed out to me that it's a rude
gesture, the gesture of a barbarian."

"I agree," Cory said. "I can't believe they actually
obey you when you do that."

"As I said, it's the custom and one I hardly
expect an independent lady like you to appreciate."

"But you must not appreciate it either if you're trying to change."

"In many ways I'm just as primitive as the El Zabor." He smiled cynically. "And sometimes it's a case of doing as I say not as I do."

"And do they do as you say?"

His face was suddenly shadowed with remembered pain. "Most of the time. It's only on occasion that they—" He broke off. "You wouldn't be interested." He gestured toward the table. "Sit down. You must be hungry. You barely nibbled at your food on the plane."

"I was upset. I can't eat when I'm upset." she moved toward the table, carefully avoiding his gaze. Upset and on fire and hungry for something other than food.

"Then you must be upset a hell of a lot of the time." He gazed at her moodily. "You must be a good fifteen pounds thinner than when I first knew you."

"I developed edema after Michael's birth and lost the weight then. Since then I've been on the run so much I've never put it back."

"You were ill?"

There was such sharpness in his tone that she glanced at him over her shoulder in surprise. "It could have been worse. They diagnosed it in time to start treatment at once." She made a face. "I wouldn't want to go through it again though. I don't like to feel that weak and helpless."

"No, you wouldn't." He started toward her, his gaze holding her own with a strange intensity. He stopped before her. "I'm . . . sorry," he said haltingly.

She gazed at him in bewilderment. "For what?"

"That my child caused you to become ill." His fingertips touched the hollow of her cheek with exquisite gentleness. "And that I wasn't there to help you through it."

The world seemed to be narrowing around them in a velvet web of intimacy.

Dangerous intimacy. Cory pulled her gaze away from his with something resembling panic. "You forget, I gave you no choice in the matter. It wasn't your responsibility."

"A man's woman is always his responsibility." His voice softened. "And his joy, Cory."

A stream of warmth was pouring through her that was sweeter and deeper than desire. No, she mustn't feel like this, she thought frantically. This was what she had fought against so desperately four years ago. "I'm responsible for myself."

He didn't seem to be listening as his fingers moved from caressing her cheek to her hair with the same gossamer touch. "You hair is different too. I wasn't sure I liked it at first, but now I think it suits you." His index finger twined around one bouncy curl. "Wild and alive and full of sunlight."

He was touching her only with the heat of his body and the gentleness of his hand on her hair, yet she felt more possessed and invaded than she had when he had explored her with more intimacy on the plane. She could smell the soap and aftershave clinging to him and she suddenly

wanted to move closer and be enveloped in the
scent and heat and the unusual sweetness he was
offering her. She tried to laugh. "It's more practical. I just shampoo, mousse, and forget about it."

"It smells like marigolds."

"It's the shampoo."

His fingers returned to her cheek and traced
the faint shadows beneath her eyes. "You look
tired. I didn't notice these before. You always seem
to have so much energy. Didn't you rest at all?"

"A little. I was too keyed up to sleep." Her voice
was uneven and so was the pounding of her heart.
She had to get away and break this dark spell he
was weaving around her. She took a step back. "I
believe I'm hungry." She sat down in the chair
held by the white-coated servant and reached for
her napkin, spread fanlike on the eggshell delicacy of her plate. "Could you tell them to begin
serving?"

He stood looking at her a moment, his expression enigmatic, and then slowly crossed to the
table and dropped onto the chair opposite her. He
started to snap his fingers and then stopped when
he saw the frown on her face. "So I forget," he
said sulkily. "No one is perfect."

His expression was so like Michael's when he
had been scolded for some bit of mischief that she
experienced a wave of overpowering tenderness.
She quickly lowered her lashes to veil her eyes.
"No one is perfect," she agreed. "Do you suppose
you could find a way to communicate to them

that I'm starving without treating them as if they're Pavlov's dogs?"

"I don't treat them—" He turned to the servant hovering at his elbow. "Please be so good as to serve dinner."

The man looked at him in bewilderment.

"If it wouldn't be too much trouble," Damon added politely with a ferocious scowl.

The servant hesitated, then began backing toward the door.

"A little more speed would be greatly appreciated." A dangerous softness had entered Damon's voice.

The servant's eyes widened in alarm and he bolted from the room.

Cory began to laugh helplessly, and Damon's gaze shifted back to her face as he asked silkily, "What's so amusing? I used all the right words. I was the soul of courtesy."

"That poor man . . ." Cory shook her head, her face still alight with laughter. "You knew he would react that way. It was very bad of you, Damon."

He smiled grudgingly. "Sometimes I get tired of being thought of as an insensitive barbarian and give in to the temptation to act like one. This whole dinner scene has a quality of déjà vu for me. Remind me to introduce you to Damita Bandor. You have a great deal in common."

She felt a tiny shock, and her smile faded. "A friend of yours?"

He nodded. "And the wife of my friend, Cam. She doesn't like finger-snapping either."

Why did she feel so relieved, Cory wondered. Not only relieved, but her spirits were rising like a balloon soaring into the sky. "Then she's a woman of extremely good sense."

He nodded absently, his gaze on her face. "She married Cam."

She laughed again. "And that automatically certifies her intelligence? Good Lord, that's chauvinistic."

He frowned. "I didn't mean it like that. Cameron Bandor is special. Even you would approve of him."

"Why is he special?"

He shrugged. "He just is."

"No, I really want to know." Her eyes were bright with curiosity. "Tell me."

"So that you can use him against me too?"

The question jarred through her, bringing shock and pain in its wake. Somehow she had lost touch with her original purpose and been caught up in the force of Damon's personality and the intriguing things she was learning about him. It was just as well he had reminded her, she told herself. She forced a smile. "Perhaps. Anyway, it won't hurt to tell me about Cam, will it?"

"No, I guess not." He motioned for the remaining servant in the room to fill the wineglasses, and the man sprang forward to obey. "Cam and I went to school together in France. He's one of the peacemakers of the world and he helped me survive those six years without getting expelled." He smiled grimly. "Or killing someone. It was a major accomplishment. If you think I'm a barbarian now, you should have seen me before Cam filed off some of the rough edges."

"I never called you a barbarian," she said slowly. "You're the one who always refers to yourself that way."

"Defense mechanism." He smiled crookedly. "I learned a long time ago it hurts less to call myself a savage than have someone else do it."

"Hurt?"

His head lifted proudly. "That's the wrong word. They didn't really hurt me, they only made me angry."

No, hurt had been exactly the right word, Cory thought with a sudden pang. She could visualize Damon coming from this atmosphere, where he was almost idolized, to the harshness of a world who despised not only his differences but that explosive temperament that made him all the more difficult.

"Why didn't your parents let you come back to Kasmara?"

"My mother died when I was two and my father soon after I went away to school." Damon lifted his glass to his lips. "My father had set up certain legal guardians for my trusts, but my personal guardianship was in the hands of the chieftains of the El Zabor. He knew they'd let nothing happen to me." He sipped the wine again before setting the goblet back on the table. "I could have come home if I'd wished."

"Then why didn't you?"

His hand tightened on the slender stem of the glass. "Because I knew I needed what they were teaching me. The El Zabor is mired in traditions that have no place in the modern world. I had to know what the West had to offer so I could choose what was best for them. I had responsibilities."

So he had let himself be ripped and scarred for six long years to meet those responsibilities. "There must have been some other way," she said gently.

He shook his head. "There was another reason. I'm not blind to my faults. I know I'm reckless and wild and I was even more so when I was a child. I knew I'd need the self-discipline I'd learn from them. Though Cam would claim I learned precious little, the experience did help."

She gazed at him in amazement. The simplicity with which he spoke was a story in itself. He didn't realize how remarkable it was to find a child who was capable of that kind of self-sacrifice. The El Zabor needed knowledge—so Damon had learned. The El Zabor needed Damon's self-discipline—so Damon had put himself through six years of painful humiliation to obtain it.

"I imagine it did help." She looked down into the ruby depths of the wine in her glass. "However, I find the solution a little drastic."

"I'm the *Bardono*," he said quietly. "It was necessary." He tossed down the rest of his wine and set the glass on the table. "And that's the reason I value my friend, Cam. Well, did you learn anything to hurt me?"

She had a feeling she was only hurting herself

by peeling away the layers of Damon's personality. Why else would she be feeling this aching need to comfort and protect as if he were as much her child as Michael? "I'll have to study the evidence and make a decision later," she said lightly.

"Always so cautious." For an instant Damon's expression held only wariness before he forced himself to smile. "You never give too much of yourself. I suppose I should be used to it by now. Drink your wine. I think you'll like it."

She sipped the wine. "It's very good," she said, her thoughts on what he had said. "I'm not that cautious in my relationships. I know how important it is to give." Then, as he gazed at her without speaking, she said, "I do give, dammit."

"Perhaps." He shrugged. "That wasn't my experience with you." The door opened and two servants bearing silver trays entered the room. "It's not important now. Let's forget about it."

Cory tried to forget about it during the entire course of the dinner, but his words kept popping into her mind like salt on a raw wound. Generosity of spirit had always been important to her, and the possibility that Damon found her lacking generosity stung her. It shouldn't be important what Damon thought of her, she assured herself. Whatever she had felt for him was lost now, buried by time and her resentment at his arrogance in taking Michael.

"You're very quiet." Damon lifted his coffee cup to his lips and looked at her over the rim. "And you've eaten practically nothing. I thought you said you were hungry."

"I ate enough." She was silent a moment, then suddenly blurted out, "I *do* give. Ask any of my friends. Ask my son."

"Are we back to that subject? I don't doubt you're a good friend and a wonderful mother. Neither of those two relationships poses a threat to you."

"And you do?'" she asked defiantly. "You're no emotional threat to me. Not then and certainly not now."

"No?" He set his cup back in its saucer with a decisive click, a spark of anger glittering in the depths of his eyes. "It seems the truce is over. Do you want to prove just how giving you can be?" He waved the servants out of the room. "All right, let's have a demonstration. Come here."

She sat there, gazing at him with blazing eyes.

"Come here," he repeated with dangerous softness. *"Kiran."*

She jumped up, the legs of her chair scraping on the marble tile as she pushed it back and came around to face him. She fell to her knees before him. "Is this what you want? Does this please you, Damon?"

"Hell, yes, it pleases me." His fingers toyed with the edge of the pink bandeau. "This is what I want from you." He suddenly jerked the bandeau down to bare her breasts. "This is all I'll ever want."

Pain shot through her with a force that stunned

her. She closed her eyes to keep him from seeing the idiotic tears that were brimming there. "Good," she said huskily. "For that's all I'll ever give you."

She heard him draw a deep breath as if struck by a blow. She could feel his gaze on her naked breasts and knew they were swelling with that damnable helpless response her body always gave Damon. Her heart was slamming so hard against the wall of her chest that it was almost painful. The long tense silence seemed to stretch on forever as she waited for his reprisal.

There was none.

She felt his hands, oddly clumsy and uncoordinated, on the silk of the bandeau, and then her breasts were once more covered.

She opened her eyes to look at him in surprise.

Damon's lids were lowered to hood his eyes as he said thickly, "Now that we've got that settled, I think you'd better leave."

"Leave?" she echoed blankly.

"You heard me. I don't want you tonight." He pushed his chair back, stood up, and strode across the room toward the French doors leading to the terrace.

He *did* want her, Cory thought in bewilderment. She was familiar enough with his physical responses to know when he was aroused and all the signs were definitely there.

"Why are you still here? You're dismissed." He stood with his back to her, looking out at the night sky. "I have no need for a *kiran* right now."

She rose slowly to her feet. She didn't understand this at all. Was he trying to show her how little importance she held for him even in the physical sense? "Is this a game?"

"I wish it were," he said heavily. "Then I could put all the pieces in a neat little box and forget about them. Will you get the hell out of here?"

"Gladly." She whirled around. "I certainly don't want to be here." She moved swiftly toward the door. "I'm happy you changed your mind about this *kiran* business."

He didn't turn. "I haven't changed my mind. It's only a reprieve, Cory. I'll see you in the morning. Good night."

She hesitated in the doorway. There was a painful tautness about his stance that hurt her in some mysterious fashion which she understood no more than she understood why he was doing this. "Good night."

She closed the door behind her and walked swiftly down the corridor toward her own suite.

"Damon."

It was Selim's voice at the door, but Damon didn't bother to turn around. "Come in."

"A messenger has come from Marain." Selim's voice was hesitant. "He respectfully wonders when you will honor him with a visit. It's the time of the sirocco and they wish to leave their encampment and go to the hills."

The muscles of Damon's back flinched and then

corded with tension. Damn, he didn't need this. Not now.

"Damon?"

There wasn't any use putting it off, when it had been too long already. "Send word to Marain that I'll be at his camp tomorrow afternoon and he'll be able to leave the following day."

"He'll be very grateful."

"*Damn* his gratitude," Damon said with soft violence. "I don't want to—" He broke off, his chest rising and falling with the harshness of his breathing. "Lord, I don't want to do this."

Selim was silent behind him. Neither of them spoke for a long time.

"But it will be done," Damon's voice held unutterable weariness.

"Shall I go with you?" Selim asked. "Or do you want me to stay with Cory and Michael?"

"I want you with me." Damon turned to face him. "And I'm taking Cory along."

Selim's eyes widened. "Is that wise?"

"Probably not." Damon smiled recklessly. "But she's taking your advice about plumbing the depths of my enigmatic personality to find ways to make me bleed. I'd hate to cheat her out of a big opportunity."

"I think you're already bleeding."

"Not yet." Damon moved toward the door. "I'm hurting but no blood has been drawn. However, I'm definitely in need of comfort."

"A woman? I could send for a *kadin*."

"Why should I send for a woman when I have one here?"

"You sent her away. I thought she might not have pleased you."

Full ripe breasts with taut pink nipples, tawny hair tumbling about her face in a silky riot of curls, shoulders and spine held ramrod-straight, belying the shadows of weariness beneath her eyes. It had been those shadows that had defeated and cheated him and left him alone and aching. The shadows and that damnable river of tenderness.

"She pleased me." Damon's chin lifted imperiously. "But I chose to wait." He opened the door. "There's plenty of time."

"Then what kind of comfort are you seeking?"

The comfort that he had always sought, Damon thought. The knowledge that he was no longer alone. The knowledge that there was a presence to whom he could give love and would perhaps forever banish solitude. "I thought I'd go see my son."

"It's late. He's probably asleep, Damon."

"I won't disturb him. I'll just sit by his bed for a while." An eager smile lit the somberness of his face. "I think I'd like that."

The door swung shut behind him.

Four

"It's like a picture out of *National Geographic*."
Cory's fascinated gaze wandered over the dozens
of black-and-gray-striped tents billowing under the
force of the strong, hot wind blowing across the
desert. No one appeared to be inside the tents; all
the activity seemed to be transpiring in the clear-
ing in the center of the encampment. The cloth-
ing of the men and women milling around was in
colorful contrast to the dark striped tents and the
stark brown-gold of the desert dunes surrounding
them. The men wore striped djellabas in a multitude of brilliant peacock colors, and white head-
pieces to shelter them from the strong sun, while
the women's robes were in solid shades of only
three colors, white, scarlet, and blue. The wom-
en's faces were unveiled, but their heads were
covered by long mantilla-like scarves in colors that

matched their robes. Cory leaned forward in the jeep and strained to get a better look as she noticed something peculiar in the scene. "But I don't see any children."

Damon didn't answer but Selim nodded to a large tent on the perimeter of the encampment. "The children are in the tent of learning. Damon decreed that every tribe set aside one tent and hire a teacher from the university to make sure the children receive at least four hours of tutoring every day." He shrugged. "It was the best he could do. The tribes are never in one place long enough for them to go to a regular school. There's a secondary school and a small hospital in the village near the palace for anyone willing to take advantage of them."

"I didn't see a village." She stiffened and darted a sudden glance at Damon in the driver's seat. "Is that where you're keeping Michael?"

Damon didn't answer. She wasn't sure he'd even heard her. His bearing was suddenly electric with tension as he caught sight of a tall, robed man standing by one of the smaller tents in the encampment.

Cory's puzzled gaze followed Damon's. There appeared to be nothing unusual about the man. He was perhaps in his mid-fifties, his dark beard flecked with gray, his skin seamed and weathered by the sun, and his demeanor was certainly not threatening. A broad smile creased his bearded face as he stepped forward eagerly when the jeep pulled up before the tent and Damon got out. He clasped Damon in a tremendous bear hug and broke into speech. Cory couldn't understand the words but his affection needed no translation.

Yet Damon stood stiff, frozen, his face totally without expression. Cory glanced questioningly at Selim.

Selim's face was grave. "The man's name is Raban. He's welcoming Damon to the encampment. Raban was almost a second father to Damon while he was growing up."

"Evidently their relationship has gone downhill since then," Cory said dryly as she stepped out of the jeep. "I'd say the affection is definitely one-sided now."

Selim shook his head. "Then you'd be wrong. Damon loves Raban."

"Then why—"

Damon turned abruptly back to them and Cory received a jolt of shock. Damon's face was pale beneath his tan and his eyes were tortured. "Take Cory to my tent," he said jerkily. "I have to talk to Raban."

Selim nodded. "I'll get her settled and then see Marain and the elders." He took Cory's elbow and urged her gently away from the jeep. "I'll be with you later, Damon."

"Later," Damon echoed as he turned back to Raban.

The man was still smiling, and he started to speak again as he drew Damon toward his tent.

"What's going on here? Damon didn't speak three words on the way from the palace." Cory frowned in puzzlement. "Why did he bring me along?"

"I'm not sure he knows himself." Selim didn't look at her. "As for what's going on, there's a tribal problem that Damon has to take care of."

"What kind of tribal problem?"

"Damon will tell you"—he paused—"if he wants you to know."

It was clear she wasn't going to hear anything more from Selim on the subject, Cory thought in frustration. "I take it there's a big, important secret we lowly females aren't permitted to know about."

Selim smiled faintly. "You might ask yourself why you want to know. If your only interest is in getting Michael back, why should it matter to you if Damon has problems?"

It shouldn't matter to her, she told herself. It was probably curiosity not concern that was making her seethe with exasperation and frustration. "It doesn't matter. I only wondered." She quickly changed the subject. "Why are the men dressed in all sorts of different colors and the women in only three."

"Custom," Selim said. "Unmarried women wear white and the married women wear scarlet."

"What about the women wearing blue?"

"Prostitutes." Selim said. "Every tribe has a certain number of women of pleasure. When Damon outlawed polygamy, their popularity increased enormously." He grinned. "The men of the tribes found it difficult to become accustomed to a lack of variety."

"How unfortunate." Cory's tone was abstracted as she cast a quick glance over her shoulder. Damon was entering the tent of Raban, his shoulders braced and rigid with tension. What the devil was wrong with him?

"They think so." They had stopped before a small tent set a short distance apart from the others, and Selim pulled aside the flaps, opening the tent, and stepped aside in order that Cory could precede him. "It was one of Damon's less popular edicts."

The tent was suffocatingly hot and Cory could feel the perspiration immediately bead on the back of her neck beneath her hair. No wonder everybody seemed to be milling around outside, she thought. That hot breeze was like a scourge, but at least you could breathe out in the open. "Do I have to stay in here?" she asked as she dropped down on the Karastan carpet. "I'd rather walk around the encampment. Is there any danger?"

"To Damon's woman?" Selim shook his head. "You'd get a few peculiar looks but no one would think of offering you an insult."

"Then let's go." She started to get up.

"No," Selim said. "Damon may need you here."

"Need?" she asked, puzzled.

"Want," he corrected himself quickly. "I'll have one of the women get you something cool to drink and you can rest until it's time for us to leave."

"I don't want to rest. I want to *do* something."

She shifted restlessly on the carpet. "How long will we be here anyway?"

"I don't think Damon will want to remain long after his business is finished. We'll probably go back to the palace tonight." He hesitated. "I have to leave you for a while. I have to go see Marain."

"Who's Marain?"

"He's the chieftain of the tribe. It was Marain who asked Damon to come today. The tribe is moving tomorrow. It's the time of the sirocco and they want to move to the hills where it's cooler."

"Sirocco," Cory repeated. "That's some kind of a storm, isn't it?"

Selim shook his head. "It's a strong hot wind that blows over the desert. It doesn't last too long, but, believe me, it can seem like forever."

Cory could well believe him as she remembered how that unrelenting wind had whipped her face and taken her breath on the journey here in the jeep. "Then why didn't they wait until they were settled in the foothills to send for Damon?"

"Marain wanted this business out of the way before they moved on."

"And Damon came when he crooked his finger?" Cory asked slowly. "That's strange."

"I told you Damon pays his dues." Selim's lips thinned. "And this time the payment may overflow the coffers." He started toward the entrance of the tent. "I'll be back as soon as I can. Try to make yourself comfortable."

"Tie back the flaps, will you? At least I can sit in the doorway and see what's going on."

"Right." He tied back the flaps and then strode away across the encampment and was presently lost from view among the tents.

Cory fumbled in the pocket of her jeans for her handkerchief and wiped the perspiration from her nape. Lord, it was hot, and that damn wind didn't help. It blew through the tent, striking like a burning whip on her cheeks. Perhaps it would be better to close the flaps after all. No, she decided, she'd rather have the wind than the stuffy boredom she would experience without the opening.

She stood up, crossed to the entrance of the tent, and looked out. The El Zabor appeared to be a good-natured, happy people. She saw nothing but smiles on the faces of the women by the cooking fires, and there seemed to be a good deal of horseplay among the men gathered around a yellow and black dartboard across the way. She saw a few children racing across the encampment, laughing and calling something to one another. School must be out, she thought as her lips curved in an indulgent smile. Children were the same no matter where they lived. She had seen Michael and Bettina's small daughter, Jessica, engaged in similar exuberant antics a hundred times. . . .

Then her smile faded as she felt a sudden wrenching pang. Michael. What was Michael doing now? She tore her gaze away from the children as she dropped down and settled herself cross-legged on the red and cream-colored Persian carpet. She must not think of Michael now. It hurt too damn much and she could do nothing out here in the middle of the desert about searching for him. Selim had said they would be going back to the palace tonight, and perhaps she could find out where he was when—

Damon was coming out of Raban's tent.

Cory automatically stiffened, every sense alert, but he wasn't coming toward where she was sitting. He didn't give the tent a glance but turned and started in the direction in which Selim had disappeared.

He was going to the chieftain Marain's tent, she guessed, her gaze following him curiously as he crossed the encampment. Her encounters with Damon had always been on an intimate one on one level and her emotional reaction to him had overshadowed her usual objectivity. It felt queer to be watching Damon as if he were a stranger as he mingled with the people in the center of the encampment.

But he wasn't mingling with the people, she noticed suddenly.

They were drawing aside as he passed by, bowing in respect, even smiling.

But no one touched him.

No one clapped him on the back or gave him an affectionate hug as Raban had done.

None of the men invited him to join in their game of darts.

Even the children stopped their shrieking and stood watching him with a diffidence generally foreign to the young.

Isolation. Loneliness.

If not in the name of love, perhaps in the

name of loneliness. Selim's words came back to her with a poignancy that was as unwelcome as it was intense. She would *not* feel sorry for Damon. He didn't deserve either forgiveness or sympathy, and she would close her mind and her emotions to both. She turned and gazed deliberately away from Damon to watch the men participating in the dart game.

When she glanced back, Damon had disappeared from sight.

The wind whipped across the moonlight-silvered dunes, lifting the grains of sand in wispy veils before whirling them in wild patterns, gaining more momentum every second until it seemed to Cory that it was blowing the moonlight itself.

"I'm sorry I couldn't come back sooner."

Cory jumped and then relaxed as she saw it was Selim beside her at the entrance of the tent. "You startled me." She made a face. "Everybody disappeared into their tents a few hours ago and it's been kind of eerie sitting here by myself." It had been more than eerie, she thought. Even before the people of the tribe had withdrawn to their tents she had noticed a sudden change in them, a somberness, a stillness, a waiting. She tried to smile. "I've been sitting here cross-legged so long, I feel as if I've turned into a statue of the Buddha."

"I meant to come back, but matters escalated. I hope you've been made comfortable."

"A very pretty little girl came by and gave me a

cup of herbal tea and some sort of stew. Have you eaten?"

Selim shook his head. "I'm not hungry." She couldn't see his expression in the darkness but she could sense a tension that seemed alien in him. And something else—that same somberness she'd noticed in the other people in the encampment. "Cory, I think you should know . . ."

She waited, and when he didn't continue, she asked impatiently. "Know what?"

"Something's happened." He paused. "Damon's—"

Her heart gave a panicky jerk. "Something's happened to Damon?"

"Not exactly."

She tried to ignore the relief pouring through her and drew an exasperated breath. "Selim, are you trying to provide me with an example of the cryptic East? For heaven's sake, make yourself clear."

"Damon's upset." He hesitated. "And when he's upset, he sometimes reacts impulsively."

"Upset? Why is he—"

"Fill up the jeep, Selim." Damon was still several yards away, but his voice cracked like a whip, echoing in the stillness. His movements were whiplike too—sharp, restless, explosive—as he strode toward them. "I'm getting out of here."

Selim nodded. "Right away." He started to turn away, and then hesitated. "Do you want me to stay until—"

"Yes," Damon interrupted. "I'll send a driver for you as soon as we get back to the palace." He reached out, grasped Cory's wrist, and pulled her to her feet. "Come along, Cory. Your first venture into the romantic world of the El Zabor is officially at an end."

"I don't know why you brought me here to begin with," Cory said. "All I've done is sit."

"I'm sorry you were bored," Damon snapped. "Perhaps we should stay after all. You might enjoy the spectacle. What do you think, Selim?"

"I think you both should get the hell away from here now," Selim said quietly. "You have no place here, Damon. You've done your part."

"Yes, I have." Damon's tone was bitterly self-mocking. "I've done more than my part. And I do it so well, don't I, Selim?"

"Damon—" Selim stopped and turned away. "I'll bring the jeep around." He strode away into the darkness.

Damon was silent, gazing after him, the muscles of his body taut, his grip on Cory's wrist painfully tight.

She tugged, trying to free herself. "You're hurting me."

His grip loosened but he didn't release her wrist. "Why should you be any different?" he said harshly. "I hurt—" He stopped and his grip deliberately tightened again on her wrist. "Why should I care if I hurt you? Do you care if you hurt me? Does anyone really care about anyone else? It's like dominoes. Set the chain in motion and we all fall down. Cause and effect."

The headlights of the jeep suddenly pierced the

darkness, and Selim drove up before the tent. He stepped out from behind the wheel and left the engine running as he came around to the passenger side.

Damon released her wrist and settled himself in the driver's seat before turning to Selim. "Let me know right away," he said curtly.

Selim nodded. "I will." He helped Cory into the jeep and leaned forward to fasten her seat belt, murmuring in a tone audible only to her. "Be careful."

"Good-bye, Selim." Cory felt a sudden reluctance at the thought of leaving him. At least he was a sympathetic presence and there was something about Damon's manner that made her uneasy.

Damon's foot slammed on the accelerator and the jeep leapt forward, jerking Cory against the restraint of the seat belt. "For heaven's sake, what's the hurry? We don't—" She turned to look at him and forgot what she had been about to say. The lights on the dashboard illuminated his features, and for the first time that evening she saw his expression. The skin was pulled tight over the broad bones of his face, his lips were curved in a reckless smile, and his eyes . . . She quickly looked away from those eyes that were glittering, wild, as if he were burning with a fever.

"I want to get back to Kasmara." His tone was as hard as his expression. "I want a drink and a shower." He glanced sidewise at her and smiled mockingly. "And a woman to soothe me."

It was a deliberate goad, she realized. Damon

wanted her to flare up at him, to give him something to fight against, a reason to unloose the violence that was seething just below the surface. "Perhaps you'll be able to get two out of three. However, I've never considered myself as particularly soothing."

"Then you'll learn." His hands tightened spasmodically on the steering wheel. "And there can't be a better time than tonight."

He stepped on the accelerator and the jeep raced forward, kicking up a spray of sand with the same wild force as the desert wind.

It was after midnight when they arrived back at the palace, but Damon was met immediately at the front door by a servant and handed a note. He quickly perused the note, his expression becoming even more flintlike. "A telephone call came for you." His tone was clipped as he glanced at Cory. "Koenig."

"Then why didn't the servant give *me* the message?"

"Because I might not have wanted you to have it." He smiled sardonically. "A *kiran's* outside contacts are governed by her protector."

She drew a steadying breath, trying to hold on to her temper. "Did he leave a message?"

"He wants you to call him." Damon crushed the note in his hand. "Which you will not do."

"The hell I won't." She whirled on her heel and started down the hall toward her suite. "If Gary called, it's because he needs me. I won't ignore that need because of your stupidity."

"You're very concerned about Koenig's 'needs.' " Damon's voice was so soft, Cory almost failed to catch the lethal chill underlying it.

"Yes, I am," she said curtly, giving him a backward glance. "There are some people in the world who don't live in palaces and have people groveling before them. They have problems you wouldn't even begin to understand."

He looked as if she had struck him. For a minute he didn't speak, then his face became shuttered, and his lids half-veiled the sudden flare of anger in his eyes. "How perceptive of you to realize how fortunate I am. You're right. I have no problems, no needs. I'm above all that." He turned away with barely concealed rage. "I'm the *Bardono*, aren't I? I'm not supposed to feel or have doubts or . . ." He didn't look at her as he strode down the hall in the direction of the library. "Make your damn call."

"I intend to," Cory called after him defiantly. "With or without your august permission. You can't—"

The library door slammed behind him, cutting off her words. She looked at the door, her hands clenched into fists at her sides. He was arrogant and rude and she should be furious with him. She *was* furious with him. She mustn't think of that agonizing pain she thought she had glimpsed a moment earlier. If she had hurt him, he deserved it, and she felt no remorse. Dear heaven, why did she feel as if she had thrown salt into an open wound?

And now she would be expected to bandage up Gary's wounds too, she thought wearily as she started once again down the hall.

She would take a quick bath before she placed the call and try to relax and rid herself of this case of nerves. She could have done without listening to Gary's troubles tonight. She had an idea she was going to have to contend with enough troubles of her own.

Cory replaced the telephone receiver on its cradle on the bedside table and sat looking down at it, trying to garner enough strength to get up and prepare herself for bed. She felt as sapped as she always did after one of Gary's bad sessions, and this one had been very bad.

"You look upset. Do Koenig's 'needs' always disturb you like this?"

Her gaze flew to the doorway where Damon was leaning against the jamb. He was still dressed in the same khaki shirt, trousers, and brown boots she had last seen him wearing. His dark hair was slightly rumpled, his smile cynical, and his eyes no longer held any hint of vulnerability. Those eyes were glittering, burning in his taut face as they had when they had left Marain's encampment.

She unconsciously tensed, bracing herself. "Sometimes." She stood up and automatically tightened the belt of her rose satin robe, striving to put more barriers between them. Not that the barriers would do any good, she thought wryly. In this mood Damon would incinerate anything in his path and not even know it was there. "Naturally, when someone is unhappy, you sympathize with them."

"And was Koenig unhappy when you left?" Damon asked mockingly.

"Of course." She looked directly into his eyes. "Would you mind leaving? I'm tired and I want to go to bed."

"As a matter of fact, I would mind." Damon straightened away from the doorjamb, took a step forward, and shut the door. "I decided since you were so high on fulfilling needs that you might as well take care of mine." He smiled faintly. "I told you I needed a shower, a drink, and a woman to soothe me. So far I've had only the drink."

She shook her head. "I don't think you even know what you do want, and I'm tired of being comforting. I have a few needs myself, and one of them is for rest."

"You rested all day at the encampment. Now it's time to go to work." He held up his right hand and deliberately snapped his fingers. "Come here."

She inhaled sharply. The provocation couldn't have been more blatantly aimed to hurt her pride and sense of self-worth. For a moment she couldn't believe that he had done it.

Then he snapped his fingers again. "Now," he said softly.

She gazed at him for a long moment, unmoving. Then she walked slowly across the room and stopped before him. "You want to humiliate me," she said quietly. "I'm not going to let you do that, Damon."

"We'll see," Damon said. "Unbutton my shirt."

She hesitated, and he snapped his fingers. She flinched and gritted her teeth as her fingers moved on the buttons. He smelled of wind and perspiration and musk. "It doesn't matter, you know," she said. "I'm still who I am no matter what you make me do. You can't touch that part of me."

A shadow flickered for the briefest instant over his face. "I know." He shrugged. "But that part of you isn't important to me anyway. So why should I worry? Put your hands on my chest."

Her palms touched the springy dark thatch roughing his chest, and she felt a tiny shock jolt through her. It was incredible, she thought dazedly. She was furious with him and yet still capable of experiencing sensual arousal.

His gaze narrowed on her face. "Why are you surprised? This is the part of you that belongs to me." His hands covered her own and pressed her palms hard against the muscles cording his chest, letting her feel the hard thump of his heart, the wiriness of his hair, the warmth of his flesh. "And always will."

"No!" Dammit, she sounded like a protesting virgin, she realized with annoyance. She tried to steady her voice. "I have a choice."

He moved her hands against him, rubbing them up and down on the hard wall of his chest. "As much as any of us." He smiled bitterly. "Which isn't a hell of a lot." He suddenly released her wrists and started across the room toward the arched doorway. "Come with me."

She stood there, caught off guard by the abruptness of his movement.

He paused at the archway to look back at her. "A shower," he said softly. "Second on my agenda. After that we'll move on to the last and the most pleasurable item."

"I've already had a bath."

"Pity. I'd have been glad to join you. I'm all for communal bathing, but perhaps it will be even more enjoyable if you can concentrate all your attention on bathing me." He disappeared through the archway. A minute later she heard the water in the shower running.

She tensed, staring blindly at the arched doorway. "Cory."

Damon's soft enunciation of her name failed to mask the underlying steel of the command.

She moved slowly toward the arched doorway. Damon was standing by the door of the shower stripping off the last of his clothes.

Power. Brawny, muscular thighs, wide shoulders, and buttocks that rippled with tight strength. It had been a long time since she had seen him like this, she thought. She had always loved to see Damon naked. It was arousing just to watch him move, the flexing of his muscles, the animal magnetism and sexuality that was so profound. Her glance moved down his body and her eyes suddenly widened.

Overwhelming.

He smiled mockingly. "You see how considerate I'm being? I could have made you finish undressing me, but I found I was too impatient."

"Then you can't expect me to appreciate your consideration." She jerked her gaze quickly back to his face and took a deep breath, her lungs feeling suddenly starved for air. "Consideration was never one of your strong points."

His lips tightened. "You never complained. I may have been impatient, but I was never cruel to you."

No, he had never been cruel and she had enjoyed his impatience. It had made her feel desired, even treasured. "Until now."

"The circumstances are different now. I have a tendency to return cruelty for cruelty." He held up his hand and snapped his fingers. "Come over here."

"Before this is over I'll probably break those fingers," she said through her teeth as she walked toward him. "I'm not going to forget this, Damon."

"Neither am I." He stood with his legs astride, his stance more challenging than she had ever seen it. "I intend to make sure you make it memorable." He stepped into the shower stall and the water poured over his shoulders and down his body in gleaming rivulets. "Take off your robe."

She untied the robe and let it drop to the floor.

He stood looking at her, and she saw the pulse in his temple jump and then accelerate. "It's been a long time. I thought I remembered but I didn't." He held out his hand in silent command to her. "You're more . . ."

She stepped beneath the warm spray and he closed the shower door. She felt suddenly caught, captured in intimacy, caged with him. Panic surged through her and she instinctively edged away.

"No." His hands cupped her shoulders and he drew her against his body. "Stay here." He widened his legs and drew her into the hollow of his hips.

Her lips parted in a silent gasp. Arousal. Hot, bold, relentless. She knew she was trembling, but she couldn't seem to stop. His palms slid slowly down her back to the curve of her buttocks. Suddenly he lifted her up and against him. She bit her lower lip to suppress a moan. He was rubbing her against him and she was aware only of sensation, the warm water caressing her flesh, the rough hair on Damon's chest teasing her nipples, his manhood moving against that most sensitive part of her. She couldn't breathe, she couldn't think. His chest was rising and falling as if he were running, and she could feel his excitement as if it were her own. Raw, elemental, primitive. Maybe it was her own, she thought dazedly. In moments like this she had always been conscious of a bonding between them that had frightened her. Sexuality wasn't supposed to be like this. It was too powerful, too encompassing.

Too frightening.

He lifted her higher, adjusted her upon him, then stopped.

She glanced up at him and her trembling increased.

His face was flushed, heavy, more sensual than she'd ever seen it. His eyes glazed, almost blind with hunger.

"Hold me." His voice was low, nearly guttural.

Her hands went instinctively to clasp his shoulders.

He drew a deep, harsh breath. "Now . . . here. Hold me here." He began to enter her with painstaking slowness, his teeth clenched. "Hold—me—*tight*."

Her neck arched back, her lips parting to get more air. It was so slow. Warm, hard, filling her emptiness, but maddeningly, excruciatingly slow. She instinctively flexed, trying to take more.

"That's right," he said hoarsely. "Tighter. I want to feel you holding me."

Her nails dug into his shoulders. She wouldn't ask him for more. She wouldn't let him know how much she needed him. She buried her face against his chest, her breath coming sporadically.

"Just a little more." Damon's voice was thick. "We . . . fit. You always feel so sweet around me. It's like a hot, tight hand." His hard palm cupping her bottom pressed with sudden force and it was done.

He froze.

The only sound was the spray of running water and the harsh rasp of Damon's breathing. Cory didn't feel as if she were breathing at all. Everything was suspended, as she was suspended, in this dark haze of passion.

His hands were moving down her back, down

her spine, molding her even closer against him. "Cory . . ." His tone held a thread of childlike wonder. "Mine. You're so much mine now. Can't you feel it?"

She did feel it, she felt possessed, owned, and somewhere beneath it all that curious dangerous bonding.

"Answer me." Damon's low voice held an element of bittersweet pain. "Just this once. Tell me you're mine, Cory."

Her hands tightened on his shoulders and she pressed her lips together to keep back the words of assent. Assent would be total capitulation, and she must never give him that.

He waited, and when she didn't speak she could feel the change in him. The stiffening where there had been yielding, the hardness where there had been only exquisite tenderness.

"No?" He laughed harshly. "I don't know why I expected anything else." Holding her with one arm, he opened the shower door and stepped out onto the Persian carpet. "Not that it matters. This is what matters." Then, somehow, they were lying on the carpet and Damon was thrusting, moving with blinding force, stunning passion, tearing her away from everything but this moment, this sensation, this bonding. . . .

No, not bonding. How had that thought insinuated itself into her consciousness? What she was feeling was only for the moment, nothing lasting. She would still be Cory Brandel, independent of everyone but herself when this sensual madness was over.

Then it was over, ending in a wild forging of splendor.

But the bonding remained, a golden chain glittering in the aftermath.

A chain that must be broken.

She closed her eyes, waiting for him to leave her.

He didn't move. His arms tightened around her with iron-hard force. "Come back to me, damn you."

She kept her eyes closed, unconsciously stiffening.

"Oh, no, not tonight. Don't do that to me tonight." His kiss was hard and rough on her lips, and then he was moving off her. He stood up and reached down to pull her to her feet. Her eyes opened to see him smile grimly at her. "That's not the way it's going to be, Cory."

He pulled her into the bedroom toward the wide low bed, where he stripped the jade satin sheet down, scattering the white silk pillows on the floor. He pushed her down on the bed's cushioned surface and turned away.

"Where are you going?"

"You're wet," he said in a growling tone. "It would be just like you to lie there and catch pneumonia to make me feel guilty." He disappeared once again into the bathroom.

She sat there, stunned, and abruptly wanted to laugh. It was absolutely absurd for Damon to demonstrate this sudden tenderness after what had gone on before. He had done his damnedest to force her submission. He had made love to her with a stunning force that had almost accomplished his objective. Now he was behaving with the bravado of a little boy who knew he had done wrong and wanted to make amends without admitting his guilt.

He knelt beside her, drying her with a thick white terry towel, keeping his gaze averted from her face. "Did I hurt you?" His voice was only a level above a whisper.

"No." She gazed at him curiously. "Did you want to?"

"No!" His gaze lifted swiftly to her face. "I'd never—I don't know. Maybe I did want to hurt you. Maybe I wanted someone else to hurt as much as I—" His shoulders shifted wearily.

As much as he was hurting himself, he was going to say, Cory realized with certainty. He had wanted someone to share his pain and there had been no one there to help him, so he had struck out. What had hurt him so much that he had reacted with such desperation, she wondered. She impulsively reached out and gently touched his hair. It was wet, rumpled, and standing on end. He looked oddly boyish, and she was again reminded of her son, Michael. Damon's son.

Strange. She had always thought of Michael as her child only, but now the realization hit her with renewed force that it was Damon's seed that had given her Michael. Together they had created a very special life.

He glanced up at her touch, his expression wary.

His wariness hurt her in a way she didn't want to analyze. She quickly took her hand away. "You're wet too. You'd better dry yourself." She lay down and drew the sheet up around her. "I'm not the only one who could get pneumonia."

He looked at her in surprise as he absently dabbed at his chest with the towel. "Not that you'd care." When she didn't answer, he continued with a touch of defiance, "I suppose you're angry with me?"

A surprising maternal tenderness surged through her. It was ridiculous to feel like this about the blasted man. He was fully mature, not a child, and this emotion was more dangerous than the passion that had gone before. "Very angry."

He looked as if she had slapped him. Well, what did the idiot expect, she wondered in exasperation. He had behaved like a wild man, and she was not about to forgive him. "Oh, for heaven's sake, come to bed and let's go to sleep."

"What?"

The words had surprised Cory as much as they had Damon. She had meant to tell him to go, to leave her. Yet the invitation to stay had tumbled out. The impulse undoubtedly had been instigated by that pain and desperation she sensed beneath every action he'd taken. For some reason she didn't want to think about him being alone with his pain tonight. She turned away from him and furiously plumped up her pillow. "You heard me."

He sat down on the edge of the bed, and she could feel him looking at her. Then he slowly reclined on the bed, lying on his back. Not touching her. Not speaking. Just lying there.

It was a long time before he spoke, and when he did, the words came haltingly, "Will you answer a question?"

She stiffened. "It depends on the question."

"Was it really because you thought I wouldn't be a good father to Michael that you left me?"

She could hurt him. She could punish him for taking Michael and all that had come after. She could do all that with one word.

She couldn't say the word. "No." She closed her eyes tightly. "Go to sleep, Damon."

"I won't sleep tonight." He put his arms under his head, gazing up at the ceiling. "Good night, Cory."

Such a conventional word to end a tempest-torn evening, she thought. She wasn't at all sure it would be even a semblance of a good night for either of them. Because Damon was lying as stiff and still as if chained and extended on a torturer's rack, and she knew he had spoken the truth when he had said he would not sleep tonight.

Five

Cory must have dozed off sometime during the night, because when she opened her eyes it was with a jarring sense of alarm.

"Michael . . ." She jerked straight up in bed, her gaze flying around the room, searching the darkness. "Michael!"

"Michael's fine." It was Damon's voice from across the room, and she saw him now, standing in front of one of the lattice-shuttered windows gazing out into the darkness through one of the intricately carved openings in the design. "You must have been dreaming."

She hadn't been dreaming, she thought hazily. It was when she had awakened that she had felt an overpowering sense of sorrow, an agony of intense emotion. Her maternal instincts had automatically connected it with Michael, but now she realized those waves of sorrow were coming from Damon.

She brushed the hair from her face and sat staring at him. He was dressed once again in the khaki shirt and sand-colored jeans and she could see the outline of his strong buttocks and wide shoulders against the white of the shutters. His spine was rigid, taut with a tension that was almost unbearable. "What are you looking at?"

"Nothing." His finger reached out and touched the smooth inner edge of the fretwork opening of one of the palm designs. "You can't see much through these windows, can you? Just glimpses, only half the view."

"Maybe that was the idea," Cory said. "Maybe if the woman who lived here were given the entire picture, she would never have stayed a prisoner."

"Perhaps." Damon didn't turn around. "Or it could be that she was content to see only the small slice she was given. It can be a great comfort not to see more than you want to see."

He was talking about something more than a mere view from the window, she realized. The undercurrents of pain she had felt before were rising and she was sensitive to them to a degree that startled her. Only with Michael had she had that close linking of emotions.

It didn't mean anything, she assured herself quickly. It was probably only the aftermath of her acceptance that Damon was just as much a part of Michael as she was. Still, since the link was there, it would do no harm to try to lessen his pain.

"Would you like to talk?" she asked quietly. "Sometimes it helps."

"Not now. It's not over yet." He was silent a moment. "Thank you for not sending me away."

"Would you have gone?"

"Probably not. I needed to be with you." He paused. "But it feels better like this."

"Why don't you come back to bed?"

"I can't relax." He shifted restlessly. "Go back to sleep."

She gazed at him helplessly for a moment before settling back on the pillows. She turned to face him again, tucking her hand beneath her cheek. She was once again conscious of the tortured tension of his body. She knew she couldn't go back to sleep again. Not with Damon standing there so silent and alone.

Waiting.

There was a knock on the door shortly after the first pale gray light of dawn pierced the darkness.

"Selim." Damon turned swiftly away from the window. "He's the only one who would disturb me here." He strode quickly across the room and threw open the door.

The light from the hallway silhouetted Selim's slim figure and Cory quickly sat up and instinctively pulled the sheet up to cover her nudity.

The action was completely unnecessary. Selim didn't give Cory a glance. His gaze was focused entirely on Damon. "It's done."

"When?"

"Three hours ago." Selim's voice was low. "Raban sent you a message."

Damon went still.

"He said to tell you he gives you his love but not his understanding."

"My God," Damon whispered. He stood there as if he had been bludgeoned, swaying with the agony of the blow.

"Should I send any message to Marain?" Selim asked.

Damon stood there staring blindly at him, not speaking.

Selim nodded. "No message. I didn't think there would be." He started to turn away.

"No. Wait." Damon's voice was hoarse, his words halting. "Send word that he did . . . well. Tell him that I'm—" He swallowed, and it was a moment before he could go on. "Pleased."

Selim gazed at him before turning and vanishing down the hall.

"Damon," Cory said tentatively.

Damon didn't look at her. She didn't think he even heard her.

She tried again. "Is there anything I can do?"

He glanced over his shoulder and she smothered a gasp. His skin was gray, corpselike, and his eyes . . .

She had never seen such torment.

"No," he said dully. "It's already been done."

He moved jerkily, like a puppet in the hands of a clumsy child, toward the doorway. A moment later he was gone.

He hadn't bothered to close the door. She wondered if he even realized there was a door there in his haze of pain and despair. Dear heaven, what could have happened to make him look like that?

She pushed the covers aside and swung her legs to the floor. She couldn't stay here in helpless ignorance. She needed to know. She would get dressed and hunt up Selim and find out what the devil was going on.

But she was very careful not to ask herself why she needed so desperately to know.

She found Selim in the library sitting in the brass-studded-leather visitor's chair, a glass of brandy in his hand and lines of exhaustion carving deep lines beside his lips.

He looked up as she entered the room, and smiled mirthlessly. "I suppose it would be useless to wish you good morning. This isn't a good morning for any of us." He took a swallow of brandy. "And last night was even worse."

"What's this all about, Selim?" Cory came forward to stand beside the desk facing him. "I feel as if I'm wandering around in the dark."

"Sometimes darkness can be a blessing."

"Look, Selim, I'm not up to deciphering nuances this morning," she said wearily. "Just tell me what I want to know. Do I have to ask questions? All right, let's start with this Raban."

Selim took another drink. "That's a bad place to start. Raban is no longer with us."

Cory's eyes widened. "What do you mean?"

"Raban is dead."

"Oh, no," Cory whispered. "No wonder Damon is so upset. You said he loved Raban."

"He did." Selim looked down into the amber depths of his brandy in the glass. "He does."

"What happened?"

"Raban committed a crime. He was executed."

"But I don't understand." Cory gazed at him in bewilderment. "We saw him just yesterday. He wasn't under any kind of constraint. He was free. He was happy."

"Constraint wasn't necessary. Raban wouldn't have run away. He wouldn't have been happy anywhere else but with the El Zabor. He had spent all his life with them." Selim swirled the brandy in his glass. "Even if he hadn't been sure of Damon's friendship he still would have stayed."

"What did Damon have to do with this?"

"Everything," he said simply. "He's the *Bardono.*"

"*Bardono,*" Cory repeated slowly. She'd wondered what significance the word carried, and now she thought she could guess. She didn't want to know. The implications were too painful to contemplate.

"*Bardono* is the El Zabor word meaning 'judge,' " Selim told her. "It was Damon who ordered Raban's death."

"Good Lord," she said hoarsely as she swayed back against the desk. "How could he do that?"

"No one else could do it. It's one of Damon's duties, perhaps the most important one. The El

Zabor system of justice demands that all crucial disputes be settled by the sheikh. That's why they award total power to their shiekhs. So that there can be no question when judgment is made."

"But Raban was his friend."

"Closer than that," Selim said huskily. "But he was also guilty of murder."

"Murder!"

Selim nodded. "He killed his own child."

Cory's knees felt suddenly weak, and she dropped down on the edge of the desk. "He didn't look—" She stopped. Murderers didn't automatically wear the mark of Cain on their features. She had seen many men guilty of heinous crimes who appeared quite ordinary. "Why?"

"It was a girl child and the baby was born blind and crippled. She would have required the time and care of everyone in the tribe and, when she was grown, no man would pay a dowry for such a wife."

"So he killed her?" Cory felt sick.

"According to the laws under which he grew up, Raban had the right to do it. His wife and his daughter were as much his property as his tent or his horses. Damon published an edict forbidding the practice, but there are many traditionalists who believe the old ways are best. Raban was one of them."

"It's . . . horrible."

"Custom," Selim said. "In the old days only the fittest could survive the life of a bedouin and any weak ones had to be eliminated or the entire tribe might perish. When a child with insurmountable defects was born, the parents left it in the desert to die."

"And that's what happened this time?"

Selim nodded. "Marain didn't discover what had happened until four days later. The tribe had been on the move to a new encampment, and Raban left the child somewhere on the journey. Marain sent a message to Damon and they formed a search party to try to find the baby, but it was too late. The child was dead when they found her."

"And he knew he'd have to condemn Raban to death?"

"There was no question what the verdict would have to be," Selim said. "If he had shown Raban mercy, it would have been like a green light to anyone else who bore a defective child. He had to show them that in his eyes every child has value and that the crime would be punished in the same manner in which it had been committed."

"A life for a life."

"The El Zabor are still a very primitive society. It's the only yardstick they understand."

She had just remembered something else. "Damon sent a message to Marain that he had done well."

"The final sanction," Selim said. "Custom. The acknowledgment that the responsibility for the death was entirely the *Bardono's*. I didn't think Damon would be able to do it this time."

She didn't know how anyone could do it, Cory thought. Damon had been writhing in pain and he had still managed to make the acknowledgment freeing the tribesmen of guilt and taking it instead on his own shoulders.

"It wasn't fair to make him do that," she broke out with sudden fierceness. "Don't they realize what he must be going through? They just wash their hands of guilt and let Damon go through hell. It's not *fair*, dammit." Selim opened his lips to speak, and she motioned him to silence. "The El Zabor system of justice stinks. Why should Damon have to go through this? Why couldn't Marain or—"

"It's Damon's choice, Cory," Selim said gently. "He's been trained for this since childhood. It's his duty."

"Then he must be crazy to let them put him through this."

"He loves them, Cory."

"Why? I saw the way they treated him in that encampment. He was almost a pariah."

"They love him too. It's just very difficult for them to treat him as they do one another. He's the *Bardono*. His words guide their lives." His face became shadowed. "And in cases like this can take their lives."

Cory's nails dug into her palms. "It's cruel, Selim. He shouldn't have to do this."

Selim nodded. "But it's the only way he can help the El Zabor."

"What if something like this happens again?"

"Then he'll make judgment again."

"Lord, you make it sound easy. Why don't you *help* him?"

"There's nothing I can do." His gaze lifted to her face. "Why don't you? Damon won't accept comfort from me but perhaps he might from you."

Cory felt a tingle of shock, followed immediately by panic. It would be a mistake to go to Damon now. She was far too vulnerable. "It's not my responsibility."

Selim smiled sadly. "Are you washing your hands of responsibility too, Cory? That leaves him very much alone, doesn't it?"

In the name of loneliness. Isolation. Damon's pale face drawn in torment.

To hell with her own vulnerability. No one on this earth should have to go through something like this alone. She straightened away from the desk and started for the door.

Cory paused before the door of Damon's suite and drew a deep breath. This was a mistake. If she had even a particle of intelligence, she'd change her mind.

She knocked on the door.

No answer.

She knocked again.

No response.

She turned the knob and opened the door.

At first she thought he wasn't in the suite, then caught sight of him on the terrace. Damon was sitting on a cushioned cane chair gazing unseeingly out at the brilliant scarlet streaking the dawn sky.

"Damon." She stopped at the French doors, wondering how to go on. What could she say? Don't worry, Damon, everything is going to be fine and dandy? He knew better. He knew he might have to face a staggering decision like this next week, next month, or next year. He knew and accepted that terrifying possibility and no amount of reassurance was going to make him feel better about it. But she had to try to help; it was a driving force within her. "Is it all right if I come out and sit down?"

"I want to be alone."

Her hesitation vanished as relief poured through her. That response was blessedly familiar. Gary always said he wanted to be alone at the start of one of his down times. She had helped Gary, and surely she could help Damon too. "No, you don't." She walked briskly out onto the terrace and sat down on the chair facing him. "You want to talk. So do it."

His gaze lifted to her face. "You want me to bleed for you?"

She experienced a knifelike pain. Lord, did he think she was so callous she'd take advantage of the hell he was going through? "No, the truce is back in effect."

"Why?"

"Because I want to help," she said gently. "Call it a psychological quirk of mine. I *need* to help you, Damon. Let me. Please."

Damon looked away from her. "There's nothing you can do."

"I can listen. Tell me what you're feeling. Guilt?"

He didn't speak for a long, long time as the sky changed from scarlet to rose.

"Not guilt," he finally said slowly. "Raban had to die. He told me when I spoke to him that he would do it again. He believed that what he had done was right."

"Anger?"

There was another silence. "Yes, I guess I'm angry." He stopped, and then said roughly, "Hell, yes, I'm angry. This shouldn't have happened. It was senseless. Why won't they listen to me? I talk and plead and give commands and they nod their heads and go on doing what they've been doing for hundreds of years. Why can't they see it won't work anymore? It's a new world with new rules." He drew a harsh, uneven breath. "Sometimes I want to crack their heads. Raban was—"

"Tell me about Raban."

"Raban . . ." Damon paused. "Raban put me up on my first pony. I remember how he laughed when I fell off and came up spitting sand. Then he dusted me off and put me back on the pony. . . ." His words trailed off and he was silent again, remembering. "He laughed a lot. He enjoyed life." He broke off and closed his eyes. "Why couldn't he see that his little girl deserved that same joy. I would have helped. There are doctors and schools . . ."

Cory swallowed to ease the tightness of her throat. The pain Damon was feeling was tangible, reaching out and touching her with unbearable intimacy. She didn't want to go on with this. This wasn't like helping Gary. With him she could stand apart, there was an element of remoteness. With Damon there was no question of standing apart, the empathy was frighteningly complete. But she had to force herself to go on. Talking would be a catharsis for him, and Lord how he needed that cleansing. "Why didn't he come to you?"

"Pride. He was a proud man. It was his problem and that of his tribe. So he solved it." Damon lifted his lids to reveal eyes glittering with moisture. "He solved it."

She couldn't stand it. She didn't even realize she had jumped up from her chair until she had crossed the few paces separating them. Her arms were suddenly around him, pressing his face to her breasts, her fingers tangling in his hair as she rocked him back and forth in a passion of maternal tenderness. "It's all right. It will be fine." Those stupid, senseless words she had sworn she wouldn't use. But she would find a way of making them come true, she thought fiercely. She had to find a way. Damon mustn't suffer like this.

She felt him stiffen in surprise against her, then his arms closed around her with desperate strength. His face burrowed in the softness of her breasts and his voice was muffled. "I loved him, Cory. I didn't want to hurt him. Why couldn't he have understood?"

"I don't know." Her voice was low as she tenderly stroked his hair. "But it wasn't your fault. None of it was your fault. You wanted only to save lives, not take them."

"But I did." Damon's arms tightened around her. "I told them it was right. Who the hell am I to decide things like this? I'm only a man, for God's sake. I study and try to do what's right for them, but how do I *know*?"

She couldn't answer. She could only hold him and rock him and try to take away a little of the loneliness.

He didn't move from her arms for a long time, and the sun moved upward from the horizon while the sky became hard and blue.

Damon lifted his head from her breasts and slowly released her. He leaned back in his chair, automatically straightening his shoulders. "I'm fine now," he said gruffly. "You can go now."

Her arms felt suddenly empty and she quickly crossed them across her breasts. "You need sleep," she said gently. "Why don't you go to bed?"

"You didn't rest much either last night." He smiled wearily. "Thanks to me."

"I don't need much sleep." She didn't want to leave him. He was no longer in that first shock of despair, but she was still conscious of a deep sadness. "I'll stay if you like."

He became still. "You want to be with me?"

"You need someone here. I'll be—"

"I don't need anyone." His chin lifted proudly. "I'm sorry if I made you think I was some kind of weakling, but—"

"Weakling?" Cory gazed at him in disbelief. "Damon, how many people do you think could have done what you did? Not me. Not Selim. I don't think I know anyone who would have had the strength to make a decision like that."

He frowned uncertainly. "Are you telling me the truth?"

Cory stared at him in exasperation. He thought because he had shown her this brief moment of vulnerability that he had broken some cardinal rule of machismo. Heavens, men could be foolish. "I'm telling you the truth."

Relief washed over his face and he tried to hide it with a careless shrug. "You seem to be in the mood for dispensing gifts today."

"I told you that I gave. I just don't like being taken. Are you sure you'll be all right if I leave?"

He nodded.

She turned and started for the door.

"Cory."

There was a faint flush mantling his cheeks, and he spoke awkwardly. "I'm . . . grateful. I can give gifts too. What would you like?"

She frowned in puzzlement. "What do you mean?"

"Would you like a house, a car . . . anything?"

"Anything?" Cory met his gaze. "Then give me my son. Give me Michael."

Pain flashed across his face. "Anything but that, Cory. I can't give him up."

"Then you have nothing I want," she said wearily. "Forget it, Damon. I'm not going to bargain a few moments of the milk of human kindness against Michael. You needed help and I gave it. I told you I have some kind of psychological quirk."

"I can't forget it," he said fiercely. "I don't forget debts."

"Any more than you forget sins against you? You think I did wrong in not telling you about Michael. Well, maybe I should have told you. Maybe I was lying to myself about protecting him from you. And maybe I wanted only to keep him mine with no complications." She ran her fingers nervously through her hair. "I just don't know anymore." She fumbled with the doorknob. "But I do know it was wrong of ycu to take him like this. It was wrong."

Then she was running down the long hall, her eyes stinging with tears she refused to let fall. She couldn't let herself cry.

Because she wasn't sure if the tears would be for her own unhappiness or for Damon's.

Six

"I've come to take you to Michael," Selim said quietly as soon as she opened the door. A brilliant smile lit his face. "Thank heaven for small mercies. I don't like playing the hard-hearted keeper of the keys."

"Michael?" Joy surged through Cory. "Damon's letting me have Michael?" This morning when she had left Damon she had been certain he'd never relent, and now this was almost too good to be true.

Selim shook his head. "You're going too fast. He's giving you permission to visit with Michael and your friends whenever you like. But he's not bringing Michael here to live at the palace." He paused. "Not yet. He wants the boy to feel secure before he takes him away from the Langstroms."

Her sudden disappointment was instantly superseded by an upward swing of optimism. "But it's a start. At least I can see him. Where is he? At this village you were talking about?"

He nodded. "Damon gave the Langstroms a very nice house in the village." His eyes twinkled. "You look about as young as Michael right now."

"I'm excited." She hugged Selim with all her strength and then released him and hurried toward the door. "Let's go. What are we waiting for?"

The house allotted to the Langstroms was lovely. The white, flat-roofed villa possessed a multitude of long narrow windows and a courtyard paved in cool blue-and-white ceramic tiles surrounding a small graceful fountain. Yet Cory barely noticed these features.

Her gaze was fixed on the carved double doors of the front entrance.

Selim's sympathetic eyes never strayed from her face.

"I sent word you were coming; they'll be waiting for you." Selim honked the horn of the jeep as he pulled up before the steps leading to the front entrance. "I'll be back to pick you up at nine tonight, okay?"

"Okay." She scarcely heard what he said, for the doors were flying open and a small boy dressed in jeans and a red T-shirt was running down the steps. Cory jumped out of the jeep and met him on the second to the last step, her arms closing around his warm, sturdy body. "Michael," she whispered, blinking back the tears. "Oh, Michael."

But he was already wriggling away from her. "I

have a pony, Mama. Well, not yet, but I'm going to have one. Just as soon as I learn to take care of him. My daddy says I have to learn that first. And I have a new friend in the village, but Jessica thinks Saram's weird because he doesn't like girls and—"

"Take a breath, Michael." Cory sat back on her heels and just looked at him. It seemed years since she had last seen him instead of just a few days. "And Jessica is probably right. It shouldn't make any difference what sex anyone is." Her hand moved tenderly over his raven-dark curls. Oh, Lord, she loved him. "It doesn't make any difference to you that Jessica is a girl. She's still your friend."

Michael nodded. "That's what Daddy said." He skipped on like a pebble thrown on a still pond. "We came here on a real jet with velvet seats and I had all the sodas I wanted and then we changed to a helicopter. I liked the helicopter best." He hugged her again. "I have to go now. Jessica and Saram are waiting for me in the nursery." He made a face. "We're going to change that name. A nursery is for babies. Jessica thinks we should call it the transporter room like on *Star Trek*. What do you think?"

"I think you'd better get back to whatever you're going to call that room and break up the squabble that's going on between Saram and Jessica," Bettina said from the doorway, an affectionate smile on her round, freckled face. "Scat, Michael."

Michael started up the stairs and then ran back

down and gave Cory a quick, enthusiastic hug. "I missed you," he whispered.

"I missed you too." Her arms tightened around him and then she forced herself to loosen her grasp. "Come back and see me in a little while, okay? I want to hear more about your helicopter ride."

"And my pony." He had already disentangled himself from her embrace and was zooming up the stairs. "I have to tell you about my pony." Then he had disappeared through the doorway and she heard only the sound of his running footsteps.

Cory felt suddenly bereft.

"He's settled in very well," Bettina said quietly. "We all have. I can't tell you what Damon's offer has done for Carter. He's a new man."

Cory studied her friend's face and found that Carter wasn't the only one who showed signs of rebirth. Bettina looked more relaxed and contented than she'd ever seen her. "You like it here?"

"Who wouldn't?" Bettina grinned. "A beautiful house, mortgage-free. *Two* servants and Damon's even provided me with a darkroom, where I can start working again. It's like a dream come true.

Cory felt a swift surge of compassion. Her feelings toward Bettina and Carter had been mixed since she had learned they had allowed themselves to be deceived by Damon into accompanying Michael to Kasmara. Besides the resentment, she couldn't help sympathizing with their predicament. She knew Bettina desperately missed her career as a photographer, given up when Jessica was born, and that Carter had strong feelings about providing for his family. It must have seemed like a miracle to have all their problems solved with one wave of Damon's hand.

Bettina was looking at her with a touch of apprehension. "It's all right, isn't it? It's what you wanted? Damon is so good with Michael. . . ."

Cory hesitated. What the devil was the point of blaming Bettina and Carter? They were still her friends, and the knowledge that she felt they had betrayed her would hurt them, perhaps even destroy their chances of a better life here. It would do no harm to let them think everything was fine between her and Damon for the time being.

"It's what I wanted." Cory stood up and forced a smile as she started up the steps toward Bettina. "Now, tell me about this new job of Carter's. Do you think he's going to like it?"

Bettina's warm smile lit her face. "He's going to love it. It's the same thing he did at the mill without having to worry about the bureaucracy. He has to account only to Damon, and that will be easy. Carter says Damon will be fair." She linked her arm with Cory's as they went into the tiled foyer. "Of course, there's the language problem, but a surprising number of the power plant personnel speak English and Damon's provided an interpreter. . . ."

"Well?" Selim asked when she got into the jeep

that evening. "Are you satisfied that Damon isn't holding Michael in a dungeon and feeding him bread and water?"

"Worse." She smiled wryly. "He's treating everyone so well, it's positively sickening. Contentment can be a prison too. One that's nearly impossible to break out of."

"He won't spoil Michael, if that's what you're worrying about. Damon knows the value of discipline."

"Even though he doesn't practice it much in his personal life?"

"There had to be a release valve somewhere. He has an explosive nature and he can show no volatility with the El Zabor."

"Ah, yes, the *Bardono*." Cory leaned wearily back against the seat, her gaze on the palace that had just come into view. The lights illuminating the massive structure sparkled on the fountains and reflecting pools on the grounds surrounding it. Damon's *Arabian Night*s dream of a palace, a filigreed, golden prison.

Prison. The word as well as the manner in which she had connected it with Damon startled her. She was the one who was the prisoner, not Damon. But wasn't Damon a prisoner too? A prisoner of his responsibilities, a prisoner of his very love for the El Zabor? "How is he, Selim?"

"Better. Not good, but better. You helped him to get better, Cory." He glanced at her. "He wants to see you tonight. He told me to ask you to come to his suite when you returned to the palace."

Her eyes widened in surprise. "Ask?"

"That's the word he used." A faint smile tugged at Selim's lips. "I admit it surprised me, too. Are you going to go?"

Her gaze returned to the palace, which was much closer now, and correspondingly more overwhelming, more smothering.

"Yes," she said impulsively. "I'll go."

Fifteen minutes later she stood before the door of Damon's suite and wondered why she had agreed to come. Selim had said Damon was better. He didn't need her. Perhaps he had never needed her. The incident was over and she should distance herself from him. That was clear to anyone with any sense.

She knocked on the door.

"Come in."

She opened the door and gazed at Damon in surprise. He did look better, she thought with an unexplainable rush of relief. His demeanor was still grave, and the copper-bronze of his skin a shade paler, but that terrible haggardness was gone. "You look more rested. Did you sleep?"

He nodded. "Enough." He gazed at her uncertainly. "You found Michael well?"

"Very well. Very happy." She paused. "But he was happy in Meadowpark too. Children are exceptionally adaptable."

"He'll be happier here." His jaw squared obstinately. "He's staying, Cory."

"Only for the time being."

"No, forever. I can't—" He smiled crookedly. "So

much for being calm and reasonable. I swore I wouldn't let myself lose control."

"Are you losing control?" She studied him. "You've always appeared to be very much in control."

"I'm seldom in control when I'm with you. Not physically and not emotionally. You . . . churn me up."

She was surprised that he'd make that admission. She was even more surprised when she found herself admitting, "It's mutual."

"Then we should take steps to correct it."

Her brow wrinkled. "What do you mean?"

He crossed the room and stopped before her, his stance radiating that familiar half-defiant challenge. "I don't believe in unresolved relationships. They leave a bad taste in my mouth. I think we should do something about it."

"You did," she said dryly. "Isn't that what this idiotic *kiran* business is all about?"

"But that doesn't work anymore." He scowled moodily. "It's impossible for me to continue with it when I have no excuse. We've struck a balance. You deprived me of my son. But you also gave me gifts this morning. I've thought it over and decided it would no longer be fair to punish you."

He was so like a cross little boy trying to work his way through a complicated problem that she felt a smile tugging at her lips. "How kind of you," she said solemnly.

"It's not kindness, it's justice. I'd much prefer it the other way. I think—" He glared at her suspiciously. "Are you laughing at me?"

"Heaven forbid," she said in mock horror. "I wouldn't think of damaging your consequence by doing anything so crass."

"You *are* laughing at me." A reluctant smile touched his lips. "Did I sound pompous?"

"Very. But I think I'm getting used to it. Though I don't promise I won't be tempted to deflate you occasionally."

"I think I might like that. No one but Selim and Cam argue with me."

"So I would imagine. It's very bad for your character."

"Perhaps." His gaze was fixed intently on her face. "You're not angry with me anymore."

"I'm sure I will soon be in full force, but I'm too happy right now to make the effort."

"Michael makes you happy." It was a statement, not a question.

"I love him," she said simply.

"I know." There was the faintest touch of wistfulness in his face before he lifted his chin and glared at her. "It makes no difference. I won't let you take him from Kasmara. It's not sensible."

"And you're the one who decides what's sensible and what's not?"

"In Kasmara I do." He stopped and then continued with exasperation. "But you've made me wander from the subject. Unresolved relationships."

"Sorry," she said flippantly.

"As I said, I've been thinking about it, and I believe I have a solution."

"You're going to have me beheaded?"

He frowned warningly. "Cory."

"Well, it would certainly resolve the relationship."

Damon was silent, gazing at her in bewilderment. "I don't think I've ever seen you like this."

Cory didn't ever remember being like this when she was with Damon. Their relationship had always been too intense, too explosive to leave room for lightheartedness. What had made the difference? Her discovery of Damon's vulnerability, her respect for his strength, the knowledge that he had needed her? Perhaps a combination of all those factors had served to lessen her wariness. "The solution?" she prompted.

"I think we should spend time together." He rushed on. "Not in bed. That is, unless you want to. I wouldn't insist on it. I think I'd prefer we didn't make love." He stopped in surprise and the slightest hint of mischief glinted in his eyes. "Good Lord, I can't believe I'm saying this."

"Neither can I." She studied him curiously. "Just what are we supposed to be doing during this time we're spending together?"

"Talking, listening to music, playing cards." He waved his hand grandly. "I'll think of something."

"And how is this supposed to resolve anything?"

"I thought we might become friends. It seems sensible since you're the mother of my child."

Her eyes were suddenly twinkling. "Very sensible. Though I believe with most couples that comes somewhere near the beginning."

"So we skipped a few steps." His gaze held her own. "It's not too late to go back and start over."

Her amusement suddenly vanished. "It may not work, Damon. There are too many things weighted against it. I resent the hell out of your keeping Michael here without my consent."

His jaw set stubbornly. "He's mine. I have the right to have him here." He shrugged. "And since you have no intention of leaving him totally under my evil influence, you might as well remain here under more pleasant circumstances. You won't want Michael to be aware of any conflict between us." A sudden eager smile lit his face. "I think he likes me."

"He does like you. He chattered like a magpie about you all evening."

"Did he?" His smile faded. "I want you to know I won't interfere with your time with him. You won't even have to see me with him. I'll go to see him every morning and I'll have Selim drive you to the village after I come back to the palace. I think that's fair."

Selim had told her Damon had a strict sense of justice, but she hadn't dreamed he'd be this meticulous. "I think you're going a little overboard on the subject, Damon," she said with a smile. "I wouldn't object to catching a passing glance of the two of you together."

"I want you to be content with the arrangement."

She sobered. "I won't be content, but I can accept this a hell of a lot more easily than being your blasted *kiran*."

"That's enough to start with." He waved an imperious hand. "I'll do the rest."

She found to her surprise that his royal arrogance no longer irritated, only amused her. "I think friendship takes two."

"But if I work twice as hard at it, then—" She started to laugh and he smiled sheepishly. "Well, determination does move mountains."

"I think so too." Her face was alive with humor. "But I'm not a mountain."

His gaze moved over her with bold sensuality, lingering on the fullness of her breasts. "There are certain similarities, peaks to conquer, crevices to explore—" He stopped and grimaced. "I forgot. No sex."

"No sex," she agreed, trying to keep the breathlessness from her voice. She knew Damon had intended to keep sexuality out of their conversation, yet it had been such an integral part of their relationship that the reaction had been instinctive, just as the heat that had surged through her in response had also been instinctive. She turned swiftly toward the door. "I think I'll go to bed. Good night, Damon."

"Good night."

She turned suddenly to face him. "You'll be all right? You'll try to sleep?"

A sudden smile lit his face with radiance. "I'll be fine. I have some papers to go over with Selim. I'll work until I'm tired enough to sleep." He paused, and his next words came awkwardly. "Thank you for your concern."

She had been concerned, so concerned that it sent a shiver of uneasiness through her. She unconsciously squared her shoulders defensively as she met his gaze. "This doesn't change anything. I still intend to take Michael away from Kasmara."

Damon's smile vanished. "And I still intend to keep him here."

"There's one thing more I'd like to know. What about Carter and Bettina?"

"What about them?"

"You've caught them up in our affairs, disrupted their lives, even brought them to a foreign country. What if I manage to get Michael away from you? Are you just going to cut them adrift?"

He flinched. "My God, do you think I'd do a thing like that?"

"I don't know. That's why I'm asking."

"No," he said harshly. "There'd be no justice in doing that. If Carter does a good job, then he and Bettina will stay here regardless of what's between us." He glared at her. "Satisfied?"

Justice again. That iron-hard discipline that ran like a glittering thread through Damon's personality. She felt a melting deep within her and quickly lowered her lashes to veil her eyes. "Satisfied."

She turned and left the suite.

Seven

Damon's long fingers toyed with the jade chess piece. "Why did you become a television reporter?"

"I never wanted to do anything else. All the other children in school wanted to be the movie star being interviewed. I wanted to be the reporter asking the questions. "Cory glanced up with an impish grin. "Are you trying to disturb my concentration?"

Damon studied the chessboard carefully. "Perhaps. Where did you go to college?"

"Princeton." Cory knew exactly what Damon was doing and found herself amused. She couldn't remember how many times in the last three weeks Damon would get her involved in a game or lull her with music and then suddenly slip in a question with elaborate casualness.

"Who treated you like a doormat?" Damon didn't

look at her as he finally moved the jade knight on the chessboard.

"What?" Cory's gaze lifted with sudden wariness to Damon's face.

"You mentioned that someone treated you like a doormat before you met me." His voice was carefully casual. "I just wondered who it was."

"Why do you want to know?"

Damon kept his gaze lowered on the chessboard. "I thought perhaps I'd behead the bastard." He added politely, "If you don't mind."

"I don't mind," she said curtly. "But I'm afraid you're too late. The said bastard is already dead."

"You beheaded him yourself?"

"No, he died a depressingly natural death."

"Was he your lover?"

She didn't answer.

Damon glanced up sharply. "Was he?"

Cory moved her bishop. "You were my first lover, remember?"

"I know you were a virgin. It shocked the hell out of me." He added softly, "And it pleased the hell out of me."

"Typical male chauvinism."

"I never denied it." His gaze lowered to the chessboard again. "What did he mean to you?"

Cory shrugged. "Many things." She paused. "He was my father."

He went still. "Your father?"

"Lawrence Brandel, Esquire." She indicated the knight he had just shifted. "That was a dangerous move, you know."

"Was it?" he asked absently.

She nodded. "You play a very reckless game. I've noticed it before."

"And you're extremely cautious." He smiled. "Balance."

"Or chaos."

"Was it chaos living with Lawrence Brandel, Esquire?"

He was back to square one, and Cory had to admire the dratted man's persistence. He was obviously not going to give up until he had what he wanted. "No, living with my father was order personified. Everything ran on greased wheels. He saw to that."

"And you didn't like—"

"Damon, for heaven's sake, will you stop it? I don't want to talk about my father."

"I do. Why don't you?"

"Because he's not the most pleasant subject in the world."

"Does thinking about him bother you?"

She pushed her chair back from the game table and stood up. "Of course it doesn't bother me. He's not a bogeyman to me any longer. I've come to terms with how I feel about him."

"How did you feel about him? Did you hate him?"

"Damon . . ." Her hands clenched slowly into fists at her sides. "Yes, I hated him."

"Why?"

"Because he smothered me, because he took delight in trying to make me into a mindless robot without one independent thought. From the time I was a little girl until the time I left home I couldn't remember one day that wasn't spoiled by his petty tyrannies."

Damon's eyes narrowed on her face. "What about your mother?"

"What about her? She let him mold her into what he wanted her to be." She grimaced. "I can't remember her ever objecting to anything he said or did to me. He'd smashed her flat even before I was born."

"She didn't fight for you?"

"She couldn't even fight for herself. She was a scared little mouse of a woman. I don't know, maybe she even liked it. After my father died she promptly married another domineering man who keeps her firmly under his thumb."

"Are you bitter against her?"

"No." Then, as she met his gaze, she shrugged wearily. "I even tried to love her when I was a little girl, but there wasn't anything there to love. She was like a shadow. His shadow." She smiled with an effort. "Now are you satisfied? I've never seen such a curious man. You've asked so many questions lately, you must know me inside out."

His eyes suddenly sparkled with mischief. "Inside out? There's definitely a correlation. We started inside and—"

"I know exactly how we started," she said quickly. She wanted no reminders at this moment of their days of glorious eroticism. She was too tense, too wired with memories she preferred to keep at bay.

"I'm tired of playing chess. I think I'll go see Selim and find out if the helicopter brought Michael's picture books today."

"They came. I took them to the villa this morning." Damon stood up, gazing gravely at her. "Why are you running away?"

"I'm not running away. I'm just not in the mood to play chess right now."

He frowned. "You're edging away from me. Do you think I can't tell? I know you now, Cory."

"You should." She laughed brittlely. "You've asked enough questions."

"You didn't have to answer them."

"I didn't mind answering before. It's just . . ." She trailed off.

"It's just that I'm getting too close," he finished. "And you don't allow anyone to do that, do you, Cory?"

"Everyone deserves a certain amount of privacy. I don't put you through inquisitions."

"Go ahead. I'm open to any question you want to ask."

"That's not the point."

"The point is that you let me come so close and no closer. Right?"

Oh, dear, this was deteriorating into a full-fledged argument, and that wasn't what she wanted at all. These last three weeks with Damon had been so warm and free from conflict that she'd wanted them to go on forever. She had found him to be a fascinating combination of impulsiveness, arrogance, and little-boy mischief. When she would feel as maternal with him as she did with Michael, she would suddenly see a flash of that stern, grave man she had glimpsed in the encampment of the El Zabor. But in all these weeks he had never once let his guard down to reveal that other, blatantly sensual Damon who was capable of sweeping her into an erotic storm. She had never dreamed Damon could be either so companionable or so gentle. Lately she had almost come to hope that he would relent and allow her to take Michael out of Kasmara. She drew a deep breath. "I don't want to quarrel with you, Damon."

"Is a quarrel too intimate for you?" Damon asked bitterly. "Maybe you're afraid I'd violate your precious space?"

"Why are you so angry?" she asked, bewildered.

"I'm angry because you're running away again and I thought— " He gazed at her with an expression mirroring anger, frustration, and disappointment. "Never mind. I guess I'm not a patient man."

"So I've noticed." For the first time in three weeks Cory was feeling uneasy. Damon was behaving most peculiarly. This wasn't the companionable boy-man she had thought she had come to know. This was the Damon she had first met in New York. Stormy, autocratic, and volatile to a dangerous degree. "But sometimes we have to wait until matters come to a head."

"Do we?" He smiled recklessly. "I always thought it was better to initiate than wait." He started to turn away. "Will you have dinner with me tonight?"

"I was going to spend the evening at the villa."

"Change your mind." His smile deepened to beguiling sweetness. "Please."

Warmth rippled through her in a honey-golden stream. "How can I resist? It's not every day the *Bardono* says please."

"It's not every day that the *Bardono* wants his way so badly." He turned to go. "I'll make the arrangements."

"Arrangements? Are we going somewhere? Won't we have dinner here?"

He shook his head. "Not tonight. I have something special in mind."

Before she could reply, he had turned and left the library.

"Good heavens, this *is* special." Cory laughed as she stood up in the jeep to look at the small solitary black-and-gray striped tent that was dwarfed and surrounded by miles of golden dunes. "And it's certainly different." She stepped out of the jeep and looked ruefully down at her emerald chiffon gown. "However, I'm definitely overdressed. I should be wearing one of those robes I saw at the El Zabor encampment. What color do you think would be appropriate? I refuse to wear the blue, and the white or scarlet don't really fit either." She walked toward the tent, her high heels sinking into the sand with every step. "By the way, you should publish an edict banning that dress code. It's like wearing brands."

"But it makes it much simpler for the men of

the tribe." Damon's eyes twinkled. "They know exactly what's for the taking and what to leave alone. If Western societies drew such clear lines, there'd be much less misunderstanding." He glanced away from her as he lifted the flap of the tent. "And I know exactly which color you should wear."

"Really? Which?"

He didn't seem to hear her. "Do you think it's too hot to eat in here?" He gestured to the simple repast spread on a paisley silk cloth on the red and gold carpet. "I suppose we could try to transfer some of it outside."

"With this wind blowing?" Cory shook her head. "I think we'd better stay inside. It will probably cool down once the sun sets." She sat on the carpet and reached for the bottle in the ice bucket, uncorked it, and poured the wine into two glasses. "Besides, this is fun. I've never had a picnic supper in a shiekh's tent in the middle of the desert. It makes me feel quit exotic." She handed him his glass and lifted her own to her lips. "Very Lawrence of Arabia."

He frowned. "That isn't why I brought you here. I didn't want you to see anything romantic in the setting." He gazed around the stark simplicity of the interior of the tent. "That's why I told them not to bring anything but the most sparse furnishings."

Cory laughed. "I'm sorry if my reaction wasn't what you hoped. I think its very simplicity makes the exotic factor stronger." She lifted one of the aluminum tray covers. "What do we have here?" She sniffed. "Lamb, I think."

"I don't remember what I ordered." His hand tightened on the stem of the glass. "It doesn't matter."

She glanced at him over her shoulder. "You invite a lady to dinner and it doesn't matter what you feed her? How ungallant of you, Damon."

He scowled. "It's all gone wrong anyway. You weren't supposed to think everything was so damned romantic." He strode toward the tent entrance and threw open the flaps. A gust of hot wind immediately blew a thin veil of sand into the interior of the tent. "There's a sirocco blowing, it's close to a hundred degrees, and you still find everything peachy-keen."

"You don't have to sound so disgusted." She carefully covered the tray to keep the sand from blowing onto the food and sat back on her heels. "I like to try new things, and luxury isn't all that important to me." She studied him thoughtfully. "You're behaving most strangely, Damon."

"I'm trying to be fair to you, dammit." He tossed the wine in his glass onto the sand beside the tent and the red liquid first stained, and then was quickly covered by a new layer of windblown sand. "It's important that you know my life isn't only palaces. I sometimes spend months traveling among the El Zabor and live in tents like these. I get away to London and Paris occasionally and to the United States even more infrequently. I have the money to give you everything material you need, but I can't promise you that I'll ever be willing to permit you to leave me for any length of time."

She gazed at him in shock, immediately followed by a swift surge of panic. "What are you getting at, Damon?"

"I want you to marry me," he said haltingly, not looking at her. "It's the only sensible solution. We have a son each of us wants and who loves us both now. In the last weeks you've seen that I'm not always a complete savage." He stopped before adding awkwardly. "I think perhaps you might even have come to like me."

Cory's hand was trembling as she carefully set her glass on the carpet beside her. "Damon, I never thought—"

"I know." He suddenly turned to face her. "Because you never let yourself think about it. You block it out of your mind just as you block me out." He covered the few paces separating them and dropped on his knees beside her. His gaze held her own with desperate intensity. "You've liked these weeks we've spent together. I know you have. Stay with me, Cory."

She quickly shook her head. "I have a career. I have a life of my own."

"Make a new life." He reached up to touch her hair with infinite gentleness. "I'll help. I'd much rather you didn't work and just stayed with me here at Kasmara, but there's a television station in Marasef. You could work there and—"

"You have it all planned out," she said dully. "In

no time at all you'd have everything worked out exactly to your own satisfaction, wouldn't you? Everything in order and in place. . . . Your place, Damon."

The eagerness faded from his expression. "I hoped you'd think it would work out to your satisfaction too, Cory. I'd try very hard to make you happy."

"Because it would resolve the relationship?" Her lips curved in a mirthless smile. "A very 'sensible' resolution according to the great *Bardono*. You get Michael and a wife who can please you in bed. What do I get?"

"You get Michael and a husband who can please you in bed," Damon said quietly. "And a man who will try to be your friend all your life long, Cory."

"You expect me to believe you? I know you, Damon. You're one of the most autocratic men I've ever met. It's bred into your bones. How long do you think it will take for you to forget all your good intentions and revert to form. A month? A year?"

Damon's hand let go of her hair. "I expected that you would believe me. I *needed* you to believe me."

"Well, I can't." The air in the tent seemed suddenly dense, smothering. She couldn't stand it any more than she could stand the way Damon was looking at her. She jumped up. "There's too much at stake. Michael and my career and—"

"Your precious independence," Damon finished, his voice harsh.

"It *is* precious. You could never understand that."

"I'd try." He got slowly to his feet. "You never gave me a chance. You just jumped to the conclusion that I'm too much of a barbarian to realize what's important to you."

"I never said you were a barbarian."

"You never said I wasn't." He smiled bitterly. "You were always careful to straddle the fence. It was much safer not to make any decision at all. But decisions have to be made, Cory. You can put them off only so long. How well I've learned that lesson."

"I've made my decision." Cory found herself backing away from him, trying to escape. "I told you it wouldn't work."

"I could make it work."

"And smash Michael and me into the ground while you're doing it?" She shook her head. "Oh, no, Damon."

"I'd never do—" He shook his head. "I'm wasting my time, aren't I? You won't believe me no matter what I say."

"There's no use talking about it." She didn't want to talk or even think about it. The entire conversation was igniting an agony and panic that she didn't want to feel. "It just wouldn't work, Damon."

"I'm not your father, Cory."

"I know that," she said in a low voice. "You're a hell of a lot stronger." She turned and walked toward the entrance of the tent. "I want to go back to the palace now. I don't think either of us wants any dinner after this."

"I'm not giving up, Cory." He stood looking at her. "I want this marriage."

"I told you—"

"I don't care what you told me," he interrupted roughly. His eyes glittered in his suddenly taut face. "This is right, dammit."

"Because you decree that it's right?"

"No, because we—" He drew a deep breath. "You're not listening to me. You never hear what I'm trying to say to you." He smiled bitterly. "I don't know why I keep trying to convince you. I guess it's time I stopped and began to play the role you handed me. There are rewards there too. Not the ones I wanted, but beggars can't be choosers."

Even through the emotional tumult she was experiencing, Cory was conscious of the aching pain beneath Damon's bitterness. She suddenly wanted to reach out in comfort, to smooth away the pain as she had done once before. But to ease his pain she would have to leave herself more vulnerable and open than she had been since she was a child. She couldn't do that. She was already too vulnerable to Damon. She forced her gaze away from him. "Can we go now?"

He looked at her a moment, and she could sense the violent emotions seething just below the surface of his control. "Yes." He strode toward the entrance of the tent, passing her without a glance. Then he was outside and the wind was tearing at his dark hair and flattening his white shirt against his body with wild strength. He braced himself and stood there a moment as if enjoying pitting his own savage strength against the equally savage elements.

Watching him, Cory suddenly shivered with apprehension. At that moment he was like the sirocco. Strong, wild, enduring . . . and dangerous.

Then the moment was gone and he moved toward the jeep, glancing impatiently over his shoulder. "What are you waiting for? Let's get the hell out of here."

The Carrara marble sunken tub brimmed with fragrant bubbles and the water was just the right temperature. Liande had adjusted everything with her usual quiet efficiency before she left the suite.

Oh, yes, everything was always exactly right at the palace, Cory thought as she wearily leaned her head back against the foam headrest affixed to the corner of the tub.

It was strange how quickly she had become accustomed to the luxuries of Kasmara. It would probably be something of a culture shock when she got back to her tiny apartment in New York. But she wouldn't be able to go back to that apartment, she realized abruptly. She would have to go apartment hunting now that Carter and Bettina would no longer be there to care for Michael. Michael would need a garden to play in and it would be necessary to be near a good school. There would have to be adjustments to both their lives. No more foreign assignments for her for at least a few years. Michael must be made to feel secure.

She was leaving Kasmara as soon as possible.

The decision didn't really surprise her. It had been growing and blossoming ever since Damon had asked her to marry him this evening. She should have known Damon couldn't be persuaded to her way of thinking. These last weeks had been a waste of time, she thought despondently. She should have been seeking a way to get Michael away from Damon. Instead, she had spent three weeks doing nothing but pleasantly drifting.

But they had been such sweet weeks, golden weeks, full of laughter and joy and— She swiftly blocked the thought. She mustn't remember these weeks or she'd be the one to soften and be persuaded to Damon's way of thinking. And that would be the first step back into the subjugation of her childhood.

She must not be hasty. There was plenty of time to consider the possibilities of getting away from Kasmara. She must be very careful, very clever, and be sure Damon was taken by surprise. A Damon on guard would be twice as hard to overcome.

She stood up, climbed the three wide steps, and reached for the towel on the free-standing rack beside the tub. She was thinking of Damon as an enemy again. The realization generated a poignant aching somewhere deep within her. The Damon she had known these past weeks had not been an enemy. He had been part mischievous boy, part *Bardono*, part vulnerable man with all a man's doubts and uncertainties.

She tossed aside the towel, shrugged into her rose satin robe, and tied the belt at her waist. It was better if she thought of Damon as the enemy, she told herself. And, heaven above, it was certainly safer. She turned and went through the archway into the bedroom.

Damon was in her bed. The jade silken spread glowed softly against the bronze of his flesh and was pushed carelessly down until it barely covered his naked hips.

She stopped, feeling a tumult of emotion surge through her. She found surprise wasn't one of them. She knew Damon well enough to know he'd meant it when he said he wouldn't give up.

He smiled crookedly. "That was a long bath. I was getting so impatient, I was about to come in after you." His voice lowered. "You remember how I hate to wait."

She drew a deep breath and tried to stop the trembling attacking her limbs. The sexuality he had suppressed these last three weeks was now blatantly obvious in his narrowed green eyes, the dark triangle of hair thatching his muscular chest, his bold arousal evident beneath the sheet. He was lying on his side, his head resting on his hand, and he should have appeared lazy. He didn't. He looked charged, electric, and yet at the same time almost catlike in his sensuality. "I remember. I suppose it would be stupid to ask what you're doing here?"

"Very. It wouldn't be worthy of you. You're an intelligent woman. You know we closed one chapter and opened another this evening."

"But we've already read this particular book."

"You can always find new nuances in a classic." He slowly sat up in bed. "And we're definitely a classic, Cory." He smiled. "Why don't you come over here. You know you want to."

There was nothing arrogant in the statement. It was a simple statement of fact of which they were both aware. "I don't always do everything I want."

He threw aside the covers and swung his feet to the floor.

She smothered a gasp as she felt the heat tingle through her as she looked at him. Copper-bronze flesh, brawny thighs, the muscles of his stomach tight and lean, and something in his eyes that held an ancient knowledge as exciting as it was primitive.

"But this time you will," he said softly. "Because you can't do anything else. It's been too long for both of us. Do you know how many times I've wanted to take your clothes off and sink into you in these three weeks? I'd watch the quick, nervous way you move, the way your throat arches when you throw back your head and laugh." His gaze went to the pink satin of the material covering her breasts. "I'd watch the way your breasts lift and fall with every breath and imagine how they'd look sweet and naked, wanting me to touch them." His gaze lifted to her face. "You want me to touch them now, don't you?"

"Yes." Her voice was hoarse, strangled. The electricity flowing between them was thick, heavy, an irresistible web of sensuality.

He held out his hand to her. "Then let me do it. I'm not snapping my fingers tonight. The choice is yours, Cory."

There was no choice. And he knew it. He was playing on her sexuality with a skill that was familiar and yet a thousand times more powerful than she had ever known with him. "My choice." She unconsciously moistened her lips with her tongue. It could do no harm to answer his piper's call one last time. Soon she would bè gone, and she doubted if there would ever be a man who stirred her as Damon did. She had found no one in the last four years who had even come close to making her realize her own sexuality. She walked slowly across the room and stood before him.

"I do choose, Damon," she whispered.

He expelled his breath in a little rush. "Thank heaven." His hands were swiftly untying the belt of her robe. "I wasn't sure what I'd do if you said no." He parted the robe and buried his face in her breasts. His hands slid slowly around her waist, his palms caressing her. "I love to run my hands over you." His lips caught and tugged gentle at her nipple.

She gasped and felt her knees grow weak as fire shot through her. She swayed against him. His palms stroked the small of her back, rubbing slowly in little circles as his mouth enveloped her nipple and he began to suck, varying the rhythm from gentleness to strength.

She instinctively moved closer, her fingers tangling in the crispness of his hair. She couldn't breathe. The touch of his lips, his tongue . . . His hands on her back . . .

His lips moved to her other breast, and somewhere in the haze searing through her and around her she was aware of the signs of Damon's arousal. The pounding of the pulse in his temple, the harsh movement of his chest, his nostrils flaring with every breath, and hotness of his flesh against her. He was burning as she was burning.

His fingers were moving around and down her body, searching.

Cory's fingers tightened on his hair as he found what he sought and began to press, rotate, then press again.

Her neck arched back as her lips parted to take in more air. "Damon . . ."

His head lifted from her breast. "Tell me you like it." His eyes were burning, wild in his flushed face. "Tell me you want me."

"I want . . . you." Her throat was so tight she could scarcely speak.

"What else do you want?" His teeth gently nipped her left nipple that was already sensitive from his ministrations. "This?"

Fire flashed through her. "Yes."

"And this?" Two fingers plunged and began a forceful rhythm of their own.

She shuddered. "Yes."

"You want me. Not any other man. Only me."

"Only—" She broke off as the rhythm roughened and escalated until she could no longer think.

"Me," he prompted. "I want to hear you say it."

"You." Her fingers left his hair to clutch desperately at his shoulders.

"And that's the way it's always going to be." Her robe was suddenly falling to the floor and he was pulling her down on the bed, parting her legs and moving between them. He held her gaze with his own with a power that was mesmerizing. "I can't make you love *me*." He thrust deep, filling her. "But I can make you love *this*." He undulated his hips against her and she felt the abrasiveness of the hairs on his thighs brush the smoothness of hers. His palms moved over her belly, and he smiled as he felt the muscles clench beneath his touch. "I did it before and it kept you mine for four months. It will be easier now that I have you here at Kasmara." He tugged gently at the hair surrounding her womanhood. "Who knows how long I can make you want to stay?"

"Damon, I don't want—" She was bewildered. She couldn't bear for him to leave her, yet she felt captured, held immobile between his strong thighs, and the words he was speaking were making her uneasy. She felt totally possessed.

"I know what you want." The sadness in his face was superseded by recklessness. "This." He withdrew and then plunged, beginning a wild rhythm, alternating short with long, slow with fast, until she was writhing on the bed, moving against him in a chaos of fire and hunger. It was like nothing she had ever known with Damon. It was as if he were striving to dominate her with every particle of his being, dominate her with the pleasure he was giving her, control her with the movements of his body.

And sweet heaven, he was *doing* it. She was conscious only of what Damon was doing to her, for her. Possession and passion intertwined until she couldn't tell one from the other. He didn't let her think, he permitted her just to feel. She was losing herself, becoming one with him.

"Damon, no . . ." She was aware of the panic in her voice even as her hands drew him closer. "I don't want . . . this."

"You do." His voice was fierce. "You want to belong to me." His fingers moved between them and she arched up helplessly with a low cry. "You do want this."

She wanted the pleasure but not to be bound by that pleasure as he was binding her. That golden bonding was emerging from the haze of passion, shimmering, chaining her to Damon.

Her head thrashed back and forth on the pillow and she was conscious of Damon's gaze narrowed on her face watching every nuance of expression crossing her face. "Why are you so afraid?" His voice was softly seductive. "Give in to me, Cory. I'm not hurting you. This is what you want from me. You want to belong to me."

The words were hypnotic. The rhythm of pleasure he was weaving on her body was an irresistible metronome, pounding the thought into her mind as he drove his manhood into her body.

It went on for an eternity, the soft seductive words, the rhythm, the golden bonding becoming more alluring with each thrust, each word, each passing second.

"Now, love." He bent and kissed her lips, smoothing the hair from her temples. "Come to me."

The explosion that rocked through the both of them stunned her and left her trembling. She clung helplessly to him.

It was several minutes before he lifted his head and gazed down at her. His breath was still coming in short, hard gasps and his eyes were wild. "Mine," he whispered. His lips pressed her own with a gentleness that failed to veil the underlying possession. "Say it."

"No," she said desperately.

"No matter." He raised himself off her and lay down, drawing her close. "You will soon."

She had come terrifyingly close to saying it only a moment ago, she realized. Their physical joining had been so complete that those words that reaffirmed that bond had almost tumbled out. "I'd like you to leave now," she said shakily.

"No." He drew her closer and snuggled her down spoon fashion against him. "From now on we sleep together. No separate space between us." His hands cupped her breasts in his palms. "And if I feel you drifting away from me, I'll wake you and bring you back. You're going to belong to me even in sleep, Cory."

"I won't—" She inhaled sharply as his palms began to squeeze her breasts. She couldn't be becoming aroused again so soon.

"You will." His tongue rimmed her ear and his

warm breath lifted a tendril of hair at her temple with every word. "You're going to get so used to this magic between us that you won't be able to do without it. I'll be with you every minute of the day and every minute of every day you'll know I'm wanting you, wanting to give you pleasure. What happened between us before will seem tame in comparison."

"Tame? You don't know the meaning of the word." She tried to move away from him. "Please. I want you to leave."

"Then I'll just have to change your mind." He moved over her again, gazing down at her with a mixture of mockery, lust, and pain. His head slowly lowered to part her lips in a slow, sensual kiss.

Dear God, she *did* want him again, she thought despairingly. "I won't change my mind," she whispered.

"Oh, yes, love." His expression suddenly held a flintlike determination, and she was once again conscious of the strength of will that had vanquished her own only a few moments ago. "You most certainly will," he said softly.

It was several hours later when Damon fell asleep. But Cory remained awake, gazing into the darkness.

She must leave Kasmara now.

There was not going to be any time for planning as she had hoped. She must take Michael and run as far and as fast as she was capable. Damon had been too strong for her tonight. He had won the battle if not the war. Why hadn't she realized that a man who had trained himself in discipline and strength would never relent? Yet she hadn't found him relentless when she first met him. He could have shown her that same sensual mastery as he had tonight, but he hadn't chosen to do it. Was it because she hadn't been important enough to him then? Now she was the mother of his child and had gained enormously in value. She didn't know; she was so confused and frightened and only one thing was clear to her.

If she stayed, Damon would do as he'd threatened. He would make her belong to him and in so doing destroy her independence. It was as if something within her were fighting with him, betraying her time after time in a hundred different ways. Was this how her mother had felt before she had become a lifeless caracature of a woman?

No! The thought sent a bolt of panic through her. She wouldn't be like her mother. She wouldn't let Damon do that to her.

She carefully removed Damon's hands from her breasts and slid slowly toward the edge of the bed. In another moment she was on her feet, moving cautiously around the room, gathering clothes, purse, documents, and then heading swiftly toward the bathroom. As she dressed she tried to marshal her thoughts into some semblance of a plan.

Transportation. That should be no problem. All the jeeps and their keys were kept in the huge garage across the courtyard. The servants had grown accustomed to seeing her move freely about the palace and grounds for the past three weeks. Even if she were seen, there might possibly be no outcry.

Destination. Damon would probably expect her to go toward Marasef, where there was an American embassy. Instead, she would head west toward Said Ababa. The relations between Said Ababa and Sedikhan were rumored to be strained, and she doubted if they'd willingly turn her over to Damon. The road leading to Said Ababa branched off the main road a few miles before it reached the village. She would pick up Michael at the villa, backtrack to the road to Said Ababa, and hopefully be halfway to the border before Damon discovered she was gone.

Five minutes later she glided silently out of the bathroom toward the door leading to the hall.

Eight

The pounding on the door of Cory's suite jarred Damon from sleep.

"Damon." Selim opened the door and flicked on the overhead light. His usually carefully combed hair was mussed, and he was dressed in jeans and a sport shirt instead of his customary business suit. "Abdul woke me. He was uneasy and thought you should be told what's happened." He stopped. "It's Cory."

Damon had known she was gone from the moment he opened his eyes and discovered he was alone in the bed. He tried to smother the leap of sheer terror that flooded him. "What's happened to Cory?"

"She's gone." Selim went on quickly. "Abdul saw the jeep pull out of the courtyard. He knew you'd given her the run of the palace, but it seemed odd that she should be leaving in the middle of the night. He decided he should—"

"When?" Damon was out of bed and throwing on his clothes. "How long ago?"

"About fifteen minutes. She took the road north toward the village."

That went without saying. Damon knew Cory would never leave Kasmara without taking Michael. "I'll need a jeep."

"You're going after her?"

'You're damn right I'm going after her."

"I thought you would. I ordered the jeep before I left my suite. Should I call the villa and warn the Langstroms not to give up Michael to her?"

"Do you think they'd listen?" Damon smiled crookedly. "They're her friends and Michael is her son. They'd warn her and she'd bolt with Michael. If she doesn't know we're after her, she'll move fast but she won't panic." He pulled on his boots as he added grimly, "I don't want her to panic until I catch up with her."

"I want to go with you."

Damon stood up. "Why? Are you afraid I'll break her pretty neck?"

Selim made a face. "Something like that. This has an all too familiar sound. I was hoping we'd done with all this conflict. Let's just say you may need a calming influence when you find Cory. It's very bad form to break a lady's neck in front of her child."

"Come if you like," Damon said curtly as he

strode toward the door. "It won't make any difference."

"Are you sure you're doing the right thing?" Bettina's brow creased in a worried frown. "Why don't you take a few days and think this over?"

"I've thought it over." Cory fastened Michael's seat belt and gently tucked the blanket around him. "I'm leaving Kasmara."

"Mama . . ." Michael opened his eyes to gaze up at her drowsily.

"Go back to sleep, love." She pressed a quick kiss on his forehead. "We're just going for a little drive through the desert. It will be a great adventure."

"Okay." His eyes closed again. "Will Daddy . . ." His words trailed off and seconds later he was once again deeply asleep.

Bettina hugged her flowered cotton robe closer to her body. "What are you going to tell Michael when he finds out you've left Damon, Cory?" she asked quietly. "They've grown very close since we've come to Kasmara. Michael loves his father."

Cory got into the driver's seat and started the jeep. "He'll forget. He's known him for only a month."

"And will you forget too? I've never seen you as happy and relaxed as you've been since you came here."

Cory's hands tightened on the steering wheel. "I forgot him before."

"Did you?" Bettina asked dryly. "Is that why you've had all those platonic relationships with men during the last four years?"

"Bettina, please! I'm doing what's necessary."

"All right." Bettina sighed resignedly before giving Cory a quick hug. "But do drive carefully, okay? Two of my favorite people are going to be riding in this jeep."

"I will." Cory pressed on the accelerator and the jeep shot forward. "I'll be in touch as soon as I reach New York, Bettina," she shouted.

Then the jeep was out of the courtyard and Cory turned south on the main road. Soon she was skimming down the road toward the Said Ababa turnoff.

She blinked determinedly, but the sand dunes and sky persisted in blurring together. What she was doing was right in spite of Bettina's arguments, she told herself.

But Michael did love Damon.

No, she mustn't have doubts now. She must get Michael out of Kasmara and then consider the alternatives. Perhaps if she could persuade Damon to be reasonable, they could work out joint custody. Reasonable? Good heavens, hadn't she learned anything? Damon would never be reasonable about—

Lights!

Headlights piercing the darkness ahead. Two

vehicles, coming fast, from the direction of the palace.

Damon.

Her heart jerked crazily. She spun the wheel. The jeep skidded as she made a ninety-degree turn and headed back toward the village. The turnoff to Said Ababa was closed to her, but if she could make it to Marasef, perhaps—

A gunshot!

No, it was only the front tire blowing, she realized a second later. Only? Then she didn't have time to think at all as the jeep careened wildly off the road, bumping over the bordering hardpacked sand before sliding sidewise as it reached the looser sand of the dunes.

"Mama!" Michael's frightened voice beside her.

The world turned topsy-turvy. The jeep crashed over on its side like a wounded dinosaur.

Blinding pain in her temple. No, please, this mustn't happen.

Michael . . .

Darkness.

Green eyes glittered down at her. Damon's eyes, she realized hazily. He would help Michael. No matter how angry he was with her, he would keep Michael safe. "Michael . . ." Her voice was so weak she didn't think he heard it. She tried again. "Help . . . Michael."

"Michael's fine." Damon's voice was thick. "The

seat belt saved him. You were the one who hit the ground when the jeep toppled."

Michael was all right. Relief poured through her. "Thank God," she whispered.

He nodded jerkily. "Go back to sleep. The doctor said you need to rest."

"Doctor?" She turned her head to look for him. Hot needles of agony drove through her temple.

"Lie still," Damon said hoarsely. "For heaven's sake. I can't stand it."

There was something wrong about this, she thought hazily. She was the one who had been injured. Her eyes focused on green malachite columns, white sheer draperies. "I'm back at the palace."

"Yes."

"All for nothing." Her eyes closed wearily. "Michael could have been hurt and all for nothing."

She heard a low, strangled groan that sounded oddly like an animal in pain. It was Damon. No, Damon mustn't hurt. There was so much pain in the world, but it mustn't touch Damon or Michael. She had to stay awake and try to take the pain away. But her lids were suddenly too heavy to lift. She tried to reach out with her hand. "No, Damon, you mustn't—"

Then darkness returned.

When she awoke again the pain was only a dull ache behind her eyes and it was Selim who was sitting beside her bed.

"How are you?" he asked gently.

"Better." She moved her head cautiously. No hot needles. "Much better."

He turned away and poured a half glass of water from a pitcher on the bedside table and inserted a straw. "Drink this. Your mouth must feel like it's full of cotton."

She sipped at the ice water gratefully. Her mouth felt worse than if it were stuffed with cotton, she thought; her tongue was almost sticking to the roof of her mouth. "Thanks, Selim." She cautiously lifted herself to a sitting position. "Michael . . ."

Selim was instantly beside her, adjusting the pillows. "Michael was only frightened. Not a scratch."

"I know. Damon told me." Still, it was good to hear Selim's reassurance. "Where is he? Back at the villa?"

Selim shook his head. "He's been given a room here at the palace. Damon wanted him close by for the little time he has left with him."

Cory went still. "What do you mean?"

Selim sat down in his chair again. "He's letting you go back to New York. He told me to make arrangements for your departure as soon as you're able to travel. According to the doctor, that should be in no more than about two days. It was only a mild concussion." His lips twisted ruefully. "Though the way Damon acted, you would have thought you'd suffered major brain damage."

She shook her head dazedly. "I feel as confused as if I had. Why is Damon doing this? Why now?"

"If you think about it, I believe you'll be able to

come up with an answer," he said quietly. "You've learned a lot about Damon since you came to Kasmara."

"I can't seem to think at all." She pressed her fingers to her pounding temples.

"Then lie back and rest." Selim leaned back in his chair. "Damon would toss me in the fountain if he knew I'd disturbed you." He smiled innocently. "But how was I to know you'd be upset? This is what you wanted, isn't it?"

"Yes." She rubbed at her temples. "Of course it's what I want." There was something terribly, terribly wrong. She felt suddenly cast adrift on a sea of confusion and panic. "It's just . . ." She trailed off. Why was she feeling like this? She clutched desperately at a spar in that sea. It had to have something to do with Michael. There wasn't anyone else she loved enough to throw her into this depression. "Michael. I want to see Michael." She swung her legs off the bed and threw aside the covers. "I want to make sure he's all right."

"I told you—"

"I want to see for myself," she said fiercely. If she could just see Michael, this bewilderment and sense of something gone horribly wrong might go away. "Take me to him."

Selim frowned. "You shouldn't be out of bed."

She stood up. The world bucked crazily.

Selim jumped up from his chair and steadied her as she swayed. "It's three o'clock in the morning. Michael's asleep."

"I won't wake him." She clutched at Selim's

arm, willing the weakness to go away. "I need to see him, Selim."

"Very well." Selim's arm remained around her as he snatched the rose satin robe from the bottom of the bed. "Put this on."

She obediently thrust her arms into the robe and drew it over her nightgown before tying the belt.

Selim tied the belt of her robe as if she were a small child unable to dress herself. "Now, sit down while I find your slippers."

She shook her head. "I need to go now." She was getting more exhausted by the minute, and she knew her stamina was diminishing.

"Lord, you're stubborn." He shrugged helplessly. "Come on, let's go. I'll see if I can get you back to bed before you collapse."

"I won't collapse."

Selim's arm supported her waist as he led her slowly toward the door. "The hell you won't."

The halls seemed miles long and each step drained her of a little more energy. By the time Selim finally stopped in front of one of the doors in the second corridor, she was finding it difficult to remain upright. Selim cursed softly and vehemently beneath his breath as he noticed her pallor.

"One look at Michael and I take you back to bed," he said as he opened the door. "One look . . ."

There was a lamp burning on the bedside table across the room, casting a pool of light on the little boy sleeping in the big bed. Michael. She took an eager step into the room.

And Damon.

Damon was kneeling by the bed, his dark curly head resting on the pillow beside Michael's. He was sound asleep. She stopped, her gaze resting on the man and the boy. It was all right. The terrible foreboding of something wrong was gone. It had vanished the minute she had caught sight of Damon. Once before she had awakened in the night thinking her fear was for Michael and then realized it was for Damon. Tonight she had made the same mistake again. It had been some hidden worry concerning Damon that had caused her this alarm. Her gaze caressed the broad plane of his cheek, the dark lashes closed in sleep, before shifting to Michael. They were so much alike, she thought tenderly. Boyish, impulsive, loving.

Hers.

Not only Michael, but Damon. Bound to her by that golden chain that no longer seemed at all threatening.

"Are you ready to go back?" Selim asked in a low voice.

Her gaze clung to Damon's face as she slowly nodded her head.

Selim urged her gently toward the door. "I told you he was fine."

"Yes." Everything was fine. Wonderfully, beautifully fine. "I had to see for myself."

Damon's head suddenly lifted as her voice carried to him, his gaze flying toward them. He muttered a curse and was on his feet, hurrying across the room. "Selim, what the hell are you doing?"

"She wanted to see the boy."

"And you decided to give in and let her have her way." He was lifting Cory, carrying her from the room and down the hall. "I expected you to have some sense even if she doesn't."

Selim hurried after him. "She's a damn stubborn woman. You should know that."

Cory snuggled closer, her ear pressed to Damon's chest. Damon's heart throbbing, pounding with strength. Such a wonderful secure sound, she thought contentedly. Why had she been so afraid of his strength? The fear seemed a lifetime away. "Damon."

He glanced down at her. "You'll be okay. It's natural that you should feel weak. You shouldn't have gotten out of bed."

"I had to get up," she whispered.

He nodded. "Michael . . . I guess it was too much to hope that you'd believe me when I told you he wasn't hurt."

"No, not Michael." She closed her eyes. "You. It was you."

"Didn't Selim tell you? You won't have to worry anymore about me victimizing you. You're leaving Kasmara."

"No." It was a protest, but he didn't understand.

"It's true, dammit." He drew a harsh breath. "You don't have to worry any longer."

They had reached her suite and Selim quickly opened the door and then stepped aside to let them enter. Damon carried her over to the bed and carefully laid her down on the pillows and pulled the sheet up around her.

"I'm not worrying." She tried to hold back the exhaustion that was threatening. She had to talk to Damon. There was so much she had to say. She forced her lids to open. Poor Damon, she thought with a surge of tenderness. He looked so tired and unhappy. "Lie down beside me."

He stiffened. "What?"

"You're tired . . ." Her lids refused to stay open any longer. "So tired."

"For heaven's sake, she's almost out of her head and you let her go running all over the palace. I feel like drawing and quartering you, Selim."

"She seemed clear-headed enough before," Selim protested. "And determined as the devil."

She wasn't out of her head, she thought indignantly. She had never seen things with such clarity in her entire life. Everything seemed so simple. It was as if a beam of light had spread its light around her as she had stood there gazing at Damon and Michael. But it wasn't worth arguing about right now.

She would wait until she was stronger to tell Damon how much she loved him.

"I'm not going until I see Damon," Cory said flatly. "So you can just tell the servants to take the suitcases out of the helicopter and bring them back to my suite."

Selim frowned. "Damon doesn't want to see you, Cory."

"Too bad." Cory stood up and smoothed her dress around her hips. "Because I want very much to see him. He hasn't even stuck his head into my room in the last three days, and I'll be damned if I let him whisk me away from Kasmara without seeing him. I feel as if I'm being run out of town."

"You know that isn't true," Selim said quietly. "Damon's finding this parting very difficult. It's natural for a man to avoid pain if it's possible. He's already said good-bye to Michael and—"

"Then he can say good-bye to me too. Where is he?"

"The library, but you—"

She didn't hear the rest of Selim's sentence. She was already out of the suite and walking down the corridor.

A few minutes later she threw open the door of the library. "Why won't you talk to me?" she demanded as she stepped into the room.

Damon rose from the executive chair behind the desk and she could see the muscles of his shoulders tauten as if he were bracing himself. "It's not necessary. You have what you want and—"

"Do I? I'm not so sure." She came toward him. "But I intend to find out. Why are you letting us leave Kasmara?"

"What difference does it make? You're going. You can have your life just exactly as you had it before. Michael. Koenig." He grimaced. "Have you called Koenig to tell him you're rushing back to his loving arms?"

"Gary was never my lover. He's my friend."

"A friend with whom you've spent innumerable nights."

"How did you know that?" Her gaze narrowed on his face.

"The same way I knew about Michael."

"Detectives?" She shook her head. "I don't like that Damon."

"I can't do anything about that now, can I?" he said wearily. "It's all water under the bridge."

"Yes, it is." She shrugged and dismissed the subject. "Gary lost his wife and child in an auto accident. Since then he's been pretty much on the skids, and about nine months ago he tried to cut his wrists. When he needs someone to talk to, I make sure I'm there for him."

"You could have told me," he said harshly. "Do you know how often I've thought of the two of you together, his hands on you . . . ."

"Water under the bridge," she quoted back to him softly. "We've both made mistakes, Damon." She paused. "That's why I think we should stop and take another look at what we both want."

"It doesn't matter what I want. My God, I nearly killed both you and Michael."

She gazed at him in surprise. "What are you talking about? I'm the one who was driving the jeep. If the accident was anyone's fault, it was mine."

"You were trying to get away from me," he said hoarsely. "It had to be partly my fault."

"You didn't know I'd panic and bolt."

"I should have known." His eyes were haunted. "I know you, Cory. I should have realized how you'd react when I tried to . . . I knew how you'd hate the idea of being owned." He was silent a moment. "I just didn't see any other way to keep you with me. I guess I went a little crazy."

"Well, you sure scared the hell out of me," she said dryly.

"And if you stayed with me, I'd probably do it again. I'd lose control and forget what I did to you and try to keep you with me whether you wanted to stay or not." He shook his head. "Though God knows why you'd want to do that after what I did to you."

"Damon—" She looked at him with a mixture of tenderness and exasperation. "You were not responsible for that accident. I want to stay with you. Why can't you listen to me?"

"Because I can't." His eyes were tortured. "Don't you understand? I *can't*!" He strode past her and our of the library. "I don't have the right."

A moment later the sound of his footsteps faded away in the distance, but Cory stood as if rooted to the same spot.

She finally understood. All the pieces were falling neatly into place. Selim had said she knew Damon well enough now to realize what was motivating him to send her away. It was true. It was incredibly stupid of her not to have comprehended before.

Understanding was one thing. Changing Damon's mind might be next to impossible.

She suddenly turned and strode back in the direction of her suite. She *would* change his mind, dammit. But she needed time alone with him in a place where he couldn't run away as he had done just now. A desert island would be ideal, she thought ruefully.

Then her eyes brightened as a sudden thought occurred to her. Why not? She would need help, but that shouldn't be too difficult to acquire.

Her pace quickened as she went in search of Selim.

Nine

"She's gone," Selim said as soon as he walked into Damon's suite.

Damon inhaled sharply. He had been expecting it, but the news twisted inside him like a knife. "When?" he asked.

"Just now."

Damon frowned. "Why the hell didn't you go with her? I told you that—"

"I did go with her," Selim interrupted. "I dropped her off and came back."

"You know I didn't want you merely to take them to Marasef. You were supposed to escort them to New York and make sure they were settled."

"There's no 'they,' " Selim said placidly. "Only Cory."

"What?"

"Michael is still here. Well, not at the palace. Cory asked me to take him to Bettina at the villa."

Damon gazed at him, stunned. "She left Michael?"

"Only temporarily." A faint smile touched Selim's lips. "She thought he should have company since you weren't going to be here either."

Damon's hands closed into fists at his sides. "What the devil are you talking about? I'm not going anywhere."

"Then I don't know what Cory's going to do. She doesn't know how to survive in the desert and she told me not to come back." Selim shrugged. "I guess she'll just have to take her chances."

"Selim, where is Cory?" Damon enunciated every word very carefully.

"I told you. In the desert. At approximately the same location as the tent you ordered put up the night Cory was hurt."

"Why would—" Damon drew a steadying breath. "Go get her."

Selim shook his head. "Didn't you hear me? She said she was going to stay there until you came to get her yourself. I have no intention of going after her." He met Damon's gaze. "Of course, you can send someone else after her. But you know how stubborn Cory can be, and she might get hurt if they try to force her. I don't think you'd want that."

"You know damn well I couldn't let that happen."

"Yes," Selim said. "So I really think you'd better leave right away, don't you?"

Damon started for the door. "It seems I have no

choice," he said through his teeth. "Have the heli-copter ready to go when I get back."

"I think I'll wait," Selim said with a slight smile. "As I said, Cory can be a very determined lady."

He was coming.

Cory rubbed her moist palms on the skirt of her robe as she watched the jeep approaching. There was no sense in being nervous. She could either pull this off or she couldn't.

Dear heaven, she *had* to pull it off.

The jeep was so much closer now, the wheels spraying sand wildly in all directions as Damon gunned the motor. A frown was furrowing his brow and his shoulders were stiff with tension.

He drew up before the tent, jumping out of the vehicle a second after he'd switched off the igni-tion. "Cory?"

"I'm here," she called from just inside the tent. "You shouldn't have driven the jeep so fast. You weren't even wearing your seat belt. Didn't you learn anything from what happened to me?"

"I learned a hell of a lot." He strode into the tent. "I learned—" He stopped short as he saw her. "What the devil are you wearing?"

She touched the skirt of the scarlet robe. "Selim got it for me. I thought it appropriate since you obviously need reminding that you asked me to be your wife. I don't approve of labels, so look your fill. You'll never see me wear it again." She turned in a circle. "Do you like it?"

"Yes. I think you look . . ." His voice lowered. "Why are you doing this? Why the masquerade?"

"It's no masquerade." She met his gaze. "It's a come-as-what-you-want-to-be party. I want to be your wife, Damon."

He seemed stunned. "You said you wanted to stay, but I didn't think you meant marriage."

"I want the whole shebang. I want to marry you. I want to share Michael and your life and my life and the El Zabor's life and . . ." She waved an encompassing hand. "There's nothing I don't want to share with you."

"Why?"

She was silent a moment. This was the hard part. This was commitment without a safety net. "I want to hedge and evade," she said honestly. "I don't want to tell you this." She drew a deep breath and rushed on. "I love you."

He froze and then his lips curved cynically. "What wonderful things have I done to earn this sudden burst of affection? You ran away from me three days ago."

Oh, Lord, he didn't believe she was telling the truth, Cory thought desperately. "I panicked. You crowded me. You made me doubt my own strength. That's always been my worst nightmare, to meet someone with the strength to dominate me and I wouldn't be strong enough to hold my own. There were so many years when I was growing up that I wondered if I'd ever be able to withstand . . ." She trailed off as she met his gaze.

His face was expressionless, his stance rigid.

She had to break through to him, she thought despairingly. "Did you ever wonder why I kept Michael? With a career like mine it would have been easier to put him out for adoption, but there was no question that I'd ever let him go from the moment I knew I'd conceived him."

"You love children."

"I love them, but I've never thought of myself as particularly maternal. But I knew I'd love Michael. I knew I had to have him with me." Her voice lowered to a level above a whisper. "Because I couldn't allow myself to have you in my life, and Michael was your son. In a way it would be like having part of you with none of the threat." She paused. "I think I must have known even then that I loved you."

"I don't want to hear this," he said hoarsely.

"Well, you're going to hear it." She took a step closer and grasped his arms. "Listen to me, do you think this is easy for— "

"Don't touch me," he said through his teeth. "For God's sake, keep your hands off me."

She could feel the muscles of his forearms bunch beneath her palms, and she looked up into his face in surprise. "Damon . . ." His face was no longer expressionless, it was a mask of suffering. "I have to go on. This means too much to me. Do you think it's easy to ask you to marry me when you may want me only because I'm the mother of your son and you think it's so bloody sensible? You've never said you felt anything for me besides lust. Maybe you'll never tell me you love me." She gazed at him fiercely. "But you can bet I'll do everything I can to make you love me if it takes the next fifty years. There's nothing I won't—"

"I've always loved you."

She went still. "What?"

"From the first moment I saw you at that trade exposition," Damon said simply. "You were interviewing that Japanese auto mogul and I just stood there looking at you, listening to you, watching the expressions on your face. You sparkled like clear life-giving water." He paused. "And I knew that I wanted to look at nothing else for the rest of my life."

She gazed at him in bewilderment. "But you never gave me a hint."

He smiled sadly. "I'm not stupid. I realized right away that you wanted an affair, not a commitment, so I gave you what you wanted from me." He paused. "I hoped you'd eventually decide you wanted something else from me as well. But you never did. Instead, you ran away and cut me out of your life."

"And you promptly cut me out of yours."

"I'm not without pride," he said fiercely. "Since you didn't want me, I convinced myself I'd never really wanted you either." He looked down at her hands on his arms. "Let me go."

She swallowed to ease the tightness of her throat. Joy and regret were exploding through her. They had wasted so many years they might have had together. They must not waste any more. "I won't let you go. Not now. Not ever."

He jerked away from her, turned, and strode toward the entrance of the tent.

She was losing him, she thought frantically. If he went through that door, she might never see him again.

"Damon!"

He glanced over his shoulder to see her standing rigid, her eyes blazing at him across the room.

"You come back to me."

He started to shake his head, then stopped as she punched her index finger at him. "Come back here."

He blinked in surprise.

She deliberately held up her right hand and snapped her fingers. "Right now."

An expression of shocked outrage crossed his features.

"Justice," she said, meeting his gaze. "Balance."

She snapped her fingers again.

The outrage faded from Damon's face and he slowly turned and walked back toward her. "I guess you deserve your pound of flesh."

"I want more than a pound. I want all of you and I'll do my damnedest to get it." She grimaced in distaste. "But never again like this. Someday when you're at your most autocratic, I may look back on this with some kind of pleasure, but at the moment I find it hard to believe. No more finger snapping for either of us. I did it only because I couldn't think of any other way to stop you."

"You don't understand, Cory, I can't—"

"You can." Her eyes were suddenly glittering with tears. "And I do understand. It took me a little while, but I finally figured it out. I knew you wanted me. I knew you loved Michael, so it didn't make any sense that you wouldn't want to start again. At first I thought it was guilt, but then I realized that was really only the smallest part of it. You see too clearly not to realize the accident wasn't your fault. It had to be something else." She took a step closer and cradled his cheeks in her hands. She felt him tense, a shudder ran through his body. "It's because you're the *Bardono*."

He didn't answer, his eyes gazing at her in desperation.

"It's because of that damn training of yours. You *have* to be just, you *have* to be fair. If you cause pain or injury, you have to be punished. You knew you'd been responsible for upsetting me that night, and you decided somewhere in that convoluted psyche of yours that you had to be punished for my accident too.'"

The tears that had been brimming were suddenly rolling down her cheeks. "But can't you see? You're punishing me and Michael also. I don't want to be sent back to this wonderful independent life you have mapped out for me. I can map my own life, thank you. And I know you'd never crush my independence. Every time you'd try, that balance scale you have inside you would send off alarms and I'd probably have to forcibly restrain you from donning a hair shirt."

"Don't cry." His voice was muffled. He turned

his head and his lips pressed against her palm. "Please, don't cry."

"Then listen to me." She tried to steady her voice. "And love me. Please love me, Damon."

There was silence in the tent.

His lids lowered to veil his eyes. "It wouldn't be an easy life for you."

Hope leapt within her. "Life is what you make it."

"I wouldn't want to let you out of my sight. I'd try but I'll always worry about the Koenigs and be jealous of everything that takes you away from me."

"We can work it out. I've found a few possessive bones in my body, too, lately."

"The El Zabor are a big part of my life. I can't give them up."

"I know that, Damon." She gazed at him with loving exasperation. He was doing it again, laying all the disadvantages before her with scrupulous fairness so that she could make a decision. "I wouldn't want you to give up anything or anyone you love. I'll take on your El Zabor just as you'll have to accept my career." She made a face. "As long as I don't have to wear this blasted robe when I travel with you in the desert."

He lifted his gaze to reveal eyes that were suddenly sparkling with mischief. "No problem. I'd rather you wore those pink harem pajamas anyway. They're much more suitable."

"Suitable for your *kiran*?" she asked dryly.

"Suitable for my *kiran*, my *kadin*." His hand

covered hers and he brought it to the wide, hard plane of his cheek. "My wife."

"Am I to assume I've convinced you?" she asked huskily. "You're a very difficult man, Damon."

"I know. Are you sure—"

"Hush." Her fingers on his lips quickly silenced him. "I'm sure. I don't want to have to begin this all over again. Do you suppose you could manage to say something positive?"

He was holding her with exquisite delicacy, as if she would shatter if he exerted the slightest pressure. "I'm afraid to say anything," he said in a low voice. "I'm afraid you'll change your mind. I'm afraid I'll be alone again."

Her arms tightened around him. "No, I'll never let you be alone. You'll never get away from me again."

His arms suddenly crushed her to him with breathtaking force as he buried his face in her hair. "You promise?"

He sounded just like Michael, she thought tenderly, boyish and uncertain, reaching out for love. In many ways Damon *was* a little boy, but he was also the arrogant, sensual man she'd first met, the man who had become her friend here in Kasmara, and lastly the stern, lonely *Bardono*. He was all those men.

And she loved every single one of them.

"I promise," she said softly.

THE EDITOR'S CORNER

Next month's LOVESWEPTs are sure to keep you warm as the first crisp winds of autumn nip the air! Rarely do our six books for the month have a common theme, but it just so happens our October group of LOVESWEPTs all deal with characters who must come to terms with their pasts in order to learn to love from the heart again.

In **RENEGADE**, LOVESWEPT #282, Judy Gill reunites a pair of lovers who have so many reasons for staying together, but who are pulled apart by old hurts. (Both have emotional scars that haven't yet healed.) When Jacqueline Train and Renny Knight struck a deal two years earlier, neither one expected their love to flourish in a marriage that had been purely a practical arrangement. And when Renny returns to claim her, Jacqueline is filled with panic . . . and sudden hope. But with tenderness, compassion, and overwhelming love Renny teaches her that the magic they'd created before was only a prelude to their real and enduring happiness.

LOVESWEPT #283, **ON WINGS OF FLAME**, is Gail Douglas's first published romance and one that is sure to establish her as a winner in the genre. When Jed Brannen offers Kelly Flynn the job of immortalizing his uncle's beloved pet in stained glass, she knows it's just a ploy on Jed's part. He's desperate to rekindle the romance that he'd walked away from years before. He'd been her Indiana Jones, roaming the globe in search of danger, and she'd almost managed to banish the memory of his tender caresses—until he returns in search of the only woman he's ever loved. Kelly's wounded pride makes her hold back from forgiving him, but every time she runs from him, she stumbles and falls . . . right into his arms.

Fayrene Preston brings you a jewel of a book in **EMERALD SUNSHINE**, LOVESWEPT #284. Too dazzled by the bright blue Dallas sky to keep her mind on the road, heroine Kathy Broderick rides her bike smack into Paul Garth's sleek limousine! The condition of her mangled bike isn't nearly as important to Kathy, however, as the condition of her heart when Paul offers her his help—

(continued)

and then his love. But resisting this man and the passionate hunger she feels for him, she finds, is as futile as pedaling backward. Paul has a few dark secrets he doesn't know how to share with Kathy. But as in all her romances, Fayrene brings these two troubled people together in a joyous union that won't fail to touch your soul.

TUCKER BOONE, LOVESWEPT #285, is Joan Elliott Pickart at her best! Alison Murdock has her work cut out for her as a lawyer who finds delivering Tucker's inheritance—an English butler—no small task. Swearing he's no gentleman, Tucker decides to uncover Alison's playful side—a side of herself she'd buried long ago under ambition and determination. Alison almost doesn't stop to consider what rugged, handsome Tucker Boone is doing to her orderly life, until talk of the future makes her remember the past—and her vow to rise to the top of her profession. Luckily Tucker convinces her that reaching new heights in his arms is the most important goal of all!

Kay Hooper has written the romance you've all been waiting for! In **SHADES OF GRAY,** LOVESWEPT #286, Kay tells the love story of the charismatic island ruler, Andres Sereno, first introduced in **RAFFERTY'S WIFE** last November. Sara Marsh finds that loving the man who'd abducted her to keep her safe from his enemies is something as elemental to her as breathing. But when Sara sees the violent side of Andres, she can't reconcile it with the sensitive, exquisitely passionate man she knows him to be. Andres realizes that loving Sara fuels the goodness in him, fills him with urgent need. And Sara can't control the force of her love for Andres any more than he can stop himself from doing what must be done to save his island of Kadeira. Suddenly she learns that nothing appears black and white to her anymore. She can see only shades of gray . . . and all the hues of love.

Following her debut as a LOVESWEPT author with her book **DIVINE DESIGN,** published in June, Mary Kay McComas is back on the scene with her second book for us, **OBSESSION,** LOVESWEPT #287. A powerful tale of a woman overcoming the injustices of her past with the help of a man who knows her more intimately than

(continued)

any other person on earth—before he even meets her—Mary Kay weaves an emotional web of romance and desire. Esther Brite is known to the world as a famous songwriter, one half of a the husband and wife team that brought music into the lives of millions. But when her husband and son are killed in a car accident, Esther returns to her hometown, where she'd once been shunned, searching for answers to questions she isn't sure she wants to ask. Doctor Dan Jacobey has reasons of his own for seeking sanctuary in the town of Bellewood—the one place where he could feel close to the woman he'd become obsessed with—Esther Brite. Esther and Dan discover that together they are not afraid to face the demons of the past and promise each other a beautiful tomorrow.

I think you're going to savor and enjoy each of the books next month as if you were feasting on a gourmet six-course meal!

Bon appetite!

Carolyn Nichols

Carolyn Nichols
    Editor

LOVESWEPT
Bantam Books
666 Fifth Avenue
New York, NY 10103

THE HOMETOWN HUNK CONTEST

FOR EVERY WOMAN WHO HAS EVER SAID—
"I know a man who looks just like the hero of this book"
—HAVE WE GOT A CONTEST FOR YOU!

To help celebrate our fifth year of publishing LOVESWEPT we are having a fabulous, fun-filled event called THE HOMETOWN HUNK contest. We are going to reissue six classic early titles by six of your favorite authors.

> ***DARLING OBSTACLES* by Barbara Boswell**
> ***IN A CLASS BY ITSELF* by Sandra Brown**
> ***C.J.'S FATE* by Kay Hooper**
> ***THE LADY AND THE UNICORN* by Iris Johansen**
> ***CHARADE* by Joan Elliott Pickart**
> ***FOR THE LOVE OF SAMI* by Fayrene Preston**

Here, as in the backs of all July, August, and September 1988 LOVESWEPTS you will find "cover notes" just like the ones we prepare at Bantam as the background for our art director to create our covers. These notes will describe the hero and heroine, give a teaser on the plot, and suggest a scene for the cover. Your part in the contest will be to see if a great looking local man—or men, if your hometown is so blessed—fits our description of one of the heroes of the six books we will reissue.

THE HOMETOWN HUNK who is selected (one for each of the six titles) will be flown to New York via United Airlines and will stay at the Loews Summit Hotel—the ideal hotel for business or pleasure in midtown Manhattan—for two nights. All travel arrangements made by Reliable Travel International, Incorporated. He will be the model for the new cover of the book which will be released in mid-1989. The six people who send in the winning photos of their HOMETOWN HUNK will receive a pre-selected assortment of LOVESWEPT books free for one year. Please see the Official Rules above the Official Entry Form for full details and restrictions.

We can't wait to start judging those pictures! Oh, and you must let the man you've chosen know that you're entering him in the contest. After all, if he wins he'll have to come to New York.

Have fun. Here's your chance to get the cover-lover of your dreams!

Carolyn Nichols

Carolyn Nichols
Editor
LOVESWEPT
Bantam Books
666 Fifth Avenue
New York, NY 10102—0023

THE HOMETOWN HUNK CONTEST

DARLING OBSTACLES
(Originally Published as LOVESWEPT #95)
By Barbara Boswell

COVER NOTES

The Characters:

Hero:
GREG WILDER's gorgeous body and "to-die-for" good looks haven't hurt him in the dating department, but when most women discover he's a widower with four kids, they head for the hills! Greg has the hard, muscular build of an athlete, and his light brown hair, which he wears neatly parted on the side, is streaked blond by the sun. Add to that his aquamarine blue eyes that sparkle when he laughs, and his sensual mouth and generous lower lip, and you're probably wondering what woman in her right mind wouldn't want Greg's strong, capable surgeon's hands working their magic on her—kids or no kids!

Personality Traits:
An acclaimed neurosurgeon, Greg Wilder is a celebrity of sorts in the planned community of Woodland, Maryland. Authoritative, debonair, self-confident, his reputation for engaging in one casual relationship after another almost overshadows his prowess as a doctor. In reality, Greg dates more out of necessity than anything else, since he has to attend one social function after another. He considers most of the events boring and wishes he could spend more time with his children. But his profession is a difficult and demanding one—and being both father and mother to four kids isn't any less so. A thoughtful, generous, sometimes befuddled father, Greg tries to do it all. Cerebral, he uses his intellect and skill rather than physical strength to win his victories. However, he never expected to come up against one Mary Magdalene May!

Heroine:
MARY MAGDALENE MAY, called Maggie by her friends, is the thirty-two-year-old mother of three children. She has shoulder-length auburn hair, and green eyes that shout her Irish heritage. With high cheekbones and an upturned nose covered with a smattering of freckles, Maggie thinks of herself more as the girl-next-door type. Certainly, she believes, she could never be one of Greg Wilder's beautiful escorts.

Setting: The small town of Woodland, Maryland

The Story:
Surgeon Greg Wilder wanted to court the feisty and beautiful widow who'd been caring for his four kids, but she just wouldn't let him past her doorstep! Sure that his interest was only casual, and that he preferred more sophisticated women, Maggie May vowed to keep Greg at arm's length. But he wouldn't take no for an answer. And once he'd crashed through her defenses and pulled her into his arms, he was tireless—and reckless—in his campaign to win her over. Maggie had found it tough enough to resist one determined doctor; now he threatened to call in his kids and hers as reinforcements—seven rowdy snags to romance!

Cover scene:
As if romancing Maggie weren't hard enough, Greg can't seem to find time to spend with her without their children around. Stealing a private moment on the stairs in Maggie's house, Greg and Maggie embrace. She is standing one step above him, but she still has to look up at him to see into his eyes. Greg's hands are on her hips, and her hands are resting on his shoulders. Maggie is wearing a very sheer, short pink nightgown, and Greg has on wheat-colored jeans and a navy and yellow striped rugby shirt. Do they have time to kiss?

THE HOMETOWN HUNK CONTEST

IN A CLASS BY ITSELF
(Originally Published as LOVESWEPT #66)
By Sandra Brown

COVER NOTES

The Characters:

Hero:
LOGAN WEBSTER would have no trouble posing for a Scandinavian travel poster. His wheat-colored hair always seems to be tousled, defying attempts to control it, and falls across his wide forehead. Thick eyebrows one shade darker than his hair accentuate his crystal blue eyes. He has a slender nose that flairs slightly over a mouth that testifies to both sensitivity and strength. The faint lines around his eyes and alongside his mouth give the impression that reaching the ripe age of 30 wasn't all fun and games for him. Logan's square, determined jaw is punctuated by a vertical cleft. His broad shoulders and narrow waist add to his tall, lean appearance.

Personality traits:
Logan Webster has had to scrape and save and fight for everything he's gotten. Born into a poor farm family, he was driven to succeed and overcome his "wrong side of the tracks" image. His businesses include cattle, real estate, and natural gas. Now a pillar of the community, Logan's life has been a true rags-to-riches story. Only Sandra Brown's own words can describe why he is masculinity epitomized: "Logan had 'the walk,' that saddle-tramp saunter that was inherent to native Texan men, passed down through generations of cowboys. It was, without even trying to be, sexy. The unconscious roll of the hips, the slow strut, the flexed knees, the slouching stance, the deceptive laziness that hid a latent aggressiveness." Wow! And not only does he have "the walk," but he's fun

and generous and kind. Even with his wealth, he feels at home living in his small hometown with simple, hard-working, middle-class, backbone-of-America folks. A born leader, people automatically gravitate toward him.

Heroine:
DANI QUINN is a sophisticated twenty-eight-year-old woman. Dainty, her body compact, she is utterly feminine. Dani's pale, lustrous hair is moonlight and honey spun together, and because it is very straight, she usually wears it in a chignon. With golden eyes to match her golden hair, Dani is the one woman Logan hasn't been able to get off his mind for the ten years they've been apart.

Setting: Primarily on Logan's ranch in East Texas.

The Story:
Ten years had passed since Dani Quinn had graduated from high school in the small Texas town, ten years since the night her elopement with Logan Webster had ended in disaster. Now Dani approached her tenth reunion with uncertainty. Logan would be there . . . Logan, the only man who'd ever made her shiver with desire and need, but would she have the courage to face the fury in his eyes? She couldn't defend herself against his anger and hurt—to do so would demand she reveal the secret sorrow she shared with no one. Logan's touch had made her his so long ago. Could he reach past the pain to make her his for all time?

Cover Scene:
It's sunset, and Logan and Dani are standing beside the swimming pool on his ranch, embracing. The pool is surrounded by semitropical plants and lush flower beds. In the distance, acres of rolling pasture land resembling a green lake undulate into dense, piney woods. Dani is wearing a strapless, peacock blue bikini and sandals with leather ties that wrap around her ankles. Her hair is straight and loose, falling to the middle of her back. Logan has on a light-colored pair of corduroy shorts and a short-sleeved designer knit shirt in a pale shade of yellow.

THE HOMETOWN HUNK CONTEST

C.J.'S FATE
(Originally Published as LOVESWEPT #32)
By Kay Hooper

COVER NOTES

The Characters:

Hero:
FATE WESTON easily could have walked straight off an Indian reservation. His raven black hair and strong, well-molded features testify to his heritage. But somewhere along the line genetics threw Fate a curve—his eyes are the deepest, darkest blue imaginable! Above those blue eyes are dark slanted eyebrows, and fanning out from those eyes are faint laugh lines—the only sign of the fact that he's thirty-four years old. Tall, Fate moves with easy, loose-limbed grace. Although he isn't an athlete, Fate takes very good care of himself, and it shows in his strong physique. Striking at first glance and fascinating with each succeeding glance, the serious expressions on his face make him look older than his years, but with one smile he looks boyish again.

Personality traits:
Fate possesses a keen sense of humor. His heavy-lidded, intelligent eyes are capable of concealment, but there is a shrewdness in them that reveals the man hadn't needed college or a law degree to be considered intelligent. The set of his head tells you that he is proud—perhaps even a bit arrogant. He is attractive and perfectly well aware of that fact. Unconventional, paradoxical, tender, silly, lusty, gentle, comical, serious, absurd, and endearing are all words that come to mind when you think of Fate. He is not ashamed to be everything a man can be. A defense attorney by profession, one can detect a bit of frustrated actor in his character. More than anything else, though, it's the

impression of humor about him—reinforced by the elusive dimple in his cheek—that makes Fate Weston a scrumptious hero!

Heroine:
C.J. ADAMS is a twenty-six-year-old research librarian. Unaware of her own attractiveness, C.J. tends to play down her pixylike figure and tawny gold eyes. But once she meets Fate, she no longer feels that her short, burnished copper curls and the sprinkling of freckles on her nose make her unappealing. He brings out the vixen in her, and changes the smart, bookish woman who professed to have no interest in men into the beautiful, sexy woman she really was all along. Now, if only he could get her to tell him what C.J. stands for!

Setting: Ski lodge in Aspen, Colorado

The Story:
C.J. Adams had been teased enough about her seeming lack of interest in the opposite sex. On a ski trip with her five best friends, she impulsively embraced a handsome stranger, pretending they were secret lovers—and the delighted lawyer who joined in her impetuous charade seized the moment to deepen the kiss. Astonished at his reaction, C.J. tried to nip their romance in the bud—but found herself nipping at his neck instead! She had met her match in a man who could answer her witty remarks with clever ripostes of his own, and a lover whose caresses aroused in her a passionate need she'd never suspected that she could feel. Had destiny somehow tossed them together?

Cover Scene:
C.J. and Fate virtually have the ski slopes to themselves early one morning, and they take advantage of it! Frolicking in a snow drift, Fate is covering C.J. with snow—and kisses! They are flushed from the cold weather and from the excitement of being in love. C.J. is wearing a sky-blue, one-piece, tight-fitting ski outfit that zips down the front. Fate is wearing a navy blue parka and matching ski pants.

THE HOMETOWN HUNK CONTEST

THE LADY AND THE UNICORN
(Originally Published as LOVESWEPT #29)
By Iris Johansen

COVER NOTES

The Characters:

Hero:
Not classically handsome, RAFE SANTINE's blunt, craggy features reinforce the quality of overpowering virility about him. He has wide, Slavic cheekbones and a bold, thrusting chin, which give the impression of strength and authority. Thick black eyebrows are set over piercing dark eyes. He wears his heavy, dark hair long. His large frame measures in at almost six feet four inches, and it's hard to believe that a man with such brawny shoulders and strong thighs could exhibit the pantherlike grace which characterizes Rafe's movements. Rafe Santine is definitely a man to be reckoned with, and heroine Janna Cannon does just that!

Personality traits:
Our hero is a man who radiates an aura of power and danger, and women find him intriguing and irresistible. Rafe Santine is a self-made billionaire at the age of thirty-eight. Almost entirely self-educated, he left school at sixteen to work on his first construction job, and by the time he was twenty-three, he owned the company. From there he branched out into real estate, computers, and oil. Rafe reportedly changes mistresses as often as he changes shirts. His reputation for ruthless brilliance has been earned over years of fighting to the top of the economic ladder from the slums of New York. His gruff manner and hard personality hide the tender, vulnerable side of him. Rafe also possesses an insatiable thirst for knowledge that is a passion with him. Oddly enough, he has a wry sense of

humor that surfaces unexpectedly from time to time. And, though cynical to the extreme, he never lets his natural skepticism interfere with his innate sense of justice.

Heroine:
JANNA CANNON, a game warden for a small wildlife preserve, is a very dedicated lady. She is tall at five feet nine inches and carries herself in a stately way. Her long hair is dark brown and is usually twisted into a single thick braid in back. Of course, Rafe never lets her keep her hair braided when they make love! Janna is one quarter Cherokee Indian by heritage, and she possesses the dark eyes and skin of her ancestors.

Setting: Rafe's estate in Carmel, California

The Story:
Janna Cannon scaled the high walls of Rafe Santine's private estate, afraid of nothing and determined to appeal to the powerful man who could save her beloved animal preserve. She bewitched his guard dogs, then cast a spell of enchantment over him as well. Janna's profound grace, her caring nature, made the tough and proud Rafe grow mercurial in her presence. She offered him a gift he'd never risked reaching out for before—but could he trust his own emotions enough to open himself to her love?

Cover Scene:
In the gazebo overlooking the rugged cliffs at the edge of the Pacific Ocean, Rafe and Janna share a passionate moment together. The gazebo is made of redwood and the interior is small and cozy. Scarlet cushions cover the benches, and matching scarlet curtains hang from the eaves, caught back by tasseled sashes to permit the sea breeze to whip through the enclosure. Rafe is wearing black suede pants and a charcoal gray crew-neck sweater. Janna is wearing a safari-style khaki shirt-and-slacks outfit and suede desert boots. They embrace against the breathtaking backdrop of wild, crashing, white-crested waves pounding the rocks and cliffs below.

THE HOMETOWN HUNK CONTEST

CHARADE
(Originally Published as LOVESWEPT #74)
By Joan Elliott Pickart

COVER NOTES

The Characters:

Hero:
The phrase tall, dark, and handsome was coined to describe TENNES WHITNEY. His coal black hair reaches past his collar in back, and his fathomless steel gray eyes are framed by the kind of thick, dark lashes that a woman would kill to have. Darkly tanned, Tennes has a straight nose and a square chin, with—you guessed it!—a Kirk Douglas cleft. Tennes oozes masculinity and virility. He's a handsome son-of-a-gun!

Personality traits:
A shrewd, ruthless business tycoon, Tennes is a man of strength and principle. He's perfected the art of buying floundering companies and turning them around financially, then selling them at a profit. He possesses a sixth sense about business—in short, he's a winner! But there are two sides to his personality. Always in cool command, Tennes, who fears no man or challenge, is rendered emotionally vulnerable when faced with his elderly aunt's illness. His deep devotion to the woman who raised him clearly casts him as a warm, compassionate guy—not at all like the tough-as-nails executive image he presents. Leave it to heroine Whitney Jordan to discover the real man behind the complicated enigma.

Heroine:
WHITNEY JORDAN's russet-colored hair floats past her shoulders in glorious waves. Her emerald green eyes, full breasts, and long, slender legs—not to mention her peaches-

and-cream complexion—make her eye-poppingly attractive. How can Tennes resist the twenty-six-year-old beauty? And how can Whitney consider becoming serious with him? If their romance flourishes, she may end up being Whitney Whitney!

Setting: Los Angeles, California

The Story:
One moment writer Whitney Jordan was strolling the aisles of McNeil's Department Store, plotting the untimely demise of a soap opera heartthrob; the next, she was nearly knocked over by a real-life stunner who implored her to be his fiancée! The ailing little gray-haired aunt who'd raised him had one final wish, he said—to see her dear nephew Tennes married to the wonderful girl he'd described in his letters . . . only that girl hadn't existed—until now! Tennes promised the masquerade would last only through lunch, but Whitney gave such an inspired performance that Aunt Olive refused to let her go. And what began as a playful romantic deception grew more breathlessly real by the minute. . . .

Cover Scene:
Whitney's living room is bright and cheerful. The gray carpeting and blue sofa with green and blue throw pillows gives the apartment a cool but welcoming appearance. Sitting on the sofa next to Tennes, Whitney is wearing a black crepe dress that is simply cut but stunning. It is cut low over her breasts and held at the shoulders by thin straps. The skirt falls to her knees in soft folds and the bodice is nipped in at the waist with a matching belt. She has on black high heels, but prefers not to wear any jewelry to spoil the simplicity of the dress. Tennes is dressed in a black suit with a white silk shirt and a deep red tie.

THE HOMETOWN HUNK CONTEST

FOR THE LOVE OF SAMI
(Originally Published as LOVESWEPT #34)
By Fayrene Preston

COVER NOTES

Hero:
DANIEL PARKER-ST. JAMES is every woman's dream come
true. With glossy black hair and warm, reassuring blue
eyes, he makes our heroine melt with just a glance. Daniel's lean face is chiseled into assertive planes. His lips are
full and firmly sculptured, and his chin has the determined and arrogant thrust to it only a man who's sure of
himself can carry off. Daniel has a lot in common with
Clark Kent. Both wear glasses, and when Daniel removes
them to make love to Sami, she thinks he really is
Superman!

Personality traits:
Daniel Parker-St. James is one of the Twin Cities' most
respected attorneys. He's always in the news, either in the
society columns with his latest society lady, or on the
front page with his headline cases. He's brilliant and takes
on only the toughest cases—usually those that involve
millions of dollars. Daniel has a reputation for being a
deadly opponent in the courtroom. Because he's from a
socially prominent family and is a Harvard graduate, it's
expected that he'll run for the Senate one day. Distinguished-
looking and always distinctively dressed—he's fastidious
about his appearance—Daniel gives off an unassailable air
of authority and absolute control.

Heroine:
SAMUELINA (SAMI) ADKINSON is secretly a wealthy heiress. No one would guess. She lives in a converted ware-
house loft, dresses to suit no one but herself, and dabbles
in the creative arts. Sami is twenty-six years old, with

long, honey-colored hair. She wears soft, wispy bangs and has very thick brown lashes framing her golden eyes. Of medium height, Sami has to look up to gaze into Daniel's deep blue eyes.

Setting: St. Paul, Minnesota

The Story:
Unpredictable heiress Sami Adkinson had endeared herself to the most surprising people—from the bag ladies in the park she protected . . . to the mobster who appointed himself her guardian . . . to her exasperated but loving friends. Then Sami was arrested while demonstrating to save baby seals, and it took powerful attorney Daniel Parker-St. James to bail her out. Daniel was smitten, soon cherishing Sami and protecting her from her night fears. Sami reveled in his love—and resisted it too. And holding on to Sami, Daniel discovered, was like trying to hug quicksilver. . . .

Cover Scene:
The interior of Daniel's house is very grand and supremely formal, the decor sophisticated, refined, and quietly tasteful, just like Daniel himself. Rich traditional fabrics cover plush oversized custom sofas and Regency wing chairs. Queen Anne furniture is mixed with Chippendale and is subtly complemented with Oriental accent pieces. In the library, floor-to-ceiling bookcases filled with rare books provide the backdrop for Sami and Daniel's embrace. Sami is wearing a gold satin sheath gown. The dress has a high neckline, but in back is cut provocatively to the waist. Her jewels are exquisite. The necklace is made up of clusters of flowers created by large, flawless diamonds. From every cluster a huge, perfectly matched teardrop emerald hangs. The earrings are composed of an even larger flower cluster, and an equally huge teardrop-shaped emerald hangs from each one. Daniel is wearing a classic, elegant tuxedo.

LOVESWEPT® HOMETOWN HUNK CONTEST

OFFICIAL RULES

IN A CLASS BY ITSELF by Sandra Brown
FOR THE LOVE OF SAMI by Fayrene Preston
C.J.'S FATE by Kay Hooper
THE LADY AND THE UNICORN by Iris Johansen
CHARADE by Joan Elliott Pickart
DARLING OBSTACLES by Barbara Boswell

1. NO PURCHASE NECESSARY. Enter the HOMETOWN HUNK contest by completing the Official Entry Form below and enclosing a sharp color full-length photograph (easy to see details, with the photo being no smaller than 2½″ × 3½″) of the man you think perfectly represents one of the heroes from the above-listed books which are described in the accompanying Loveswept cover notes. Please be sure to fill out the Official Entry Form completely, and also be sure to clearly print on the back of the man's photograph the man's name, address, city, state, zip code, telephone number, date of birth, your name, address, city, state, zip code, telephone number, your relationship, if any, to the man (e.g. wife, girlfriend) as well as the title of the Loveswept book for which you are entering the man. If you do not have an Official Entry Form, you can print all of the required information on a 3″ × 5″ card and attach it to the photograph with all the necessary information printed on the back of the photograph as well. YOUR HERO MUST SIGN BOTH THE BACK OF THE OFFICIAL ENTRY FORM (OR 3″ × 5″ CARD) AND THE PHOTOGRAPH TO SIGNIFY HIS CONSENT TO BEING ENTERED IN THE CONTEST. Completed entries should be sent to:

BANTAM BOOKS
HOMETOWN HUNK CONTEST
Department CN
666 Fifth Avenue
New York, New York 10102–0023

All photographs and entries become the property of Bantam Books and will not be returned under any circumstances.

2. Six men will be chosen by the Loveswept authors as a HOMETOWN HUNK (one HUNK per Loveswept title). By entering the contest, each winner and each person who enters a winner agrees to abide by Bantam Books' rules and to be subject to Bantam Books' eligibility requirements. Each winning HUNK and each person who enters a winner will be required to sign all papers deemed necessary by Bantam Books before receiving any prize. Each winning HUNK will be flown via **United Airlines** from his closest United Airlines-serviced city to New York City and will stay at the ⊪Ⅼ Ꙇꞇ Hotel—the ideal hotel for business or pleasure in midtown Manhattan—for two nights. Winning HUNKS' meals and hotel transfers will be provided by Bantam Books. Travel and hotel arrangements are made by *RELIABLE TRAVEL* and are subject to availability and to Bantam Books' date requirements. Each winning HUNK will pose with a female model at a photographer's studio for a photograph that will serve as the basis of a Loveswept cover front. Each winning HUNK will receive a $150.00 modeling fee. Each winning HUNK will be required to sign an Affidavit of Eligibility and Model's Release supplied by Bantam Books. (Approximate retail value of HOMETOWN HUNK'S PRIZE: $900.00). The six people who send in a winning HOMETOWN HUNK photograph that is used by Bantam will receive free for one year each, LOVESWEPT romance paperback books published by Bantam during that year. (Approximate retail value: $180.00.) Each person who submits a winning photograph

will also be required to sign an Affidavit of Eligibility and Promotional Release supplied by Bantam Books. All winning HUNKS' (as well as the people who submit the winning photographs) names, addresses, biographical data and likenesses may be used by Bantam Books for publicity and promotional purposes without any additional compensation. There will be no prize substitutions or cash equivalents made.

3. All completed entries must be received by Bantam Books no later than September 15, 1988. Bantam Books is not responsible for lost or misdirected entries. The finalists will be selected by Loveswept editors and the six winning HOMETOWN HUNKS will be selected by the six authors of the participating Loveswept books. Winners will be selected on the basis of how closely the judges believe they reflect the descriptions of the books' heroes. Winners will be notified on or about October 31, 1988. If there are insufficient entries or if in the judges' opinions, no entry is suitable or adequately reflects the descriptions of the hero(s) in the book(s), Bantam may decide not to award a prize for the applicable book(s) and may reissue the book(s) at its discretion.

4. The contest is open to residents of the U.S. and Canada, except the Province of Quebec, and is void where prohibited by law. All federal and local regulations apply. Employees of Reliable Travel International, Inc., United Airlines, the Summit Hotel, and the Bantam Doubleday Dell Publishing Group, Inc., their subsidiaries and affiliates, and their immediate families are ineligible to enter.

5. For an extra copy of the Official Rules, the Official Entry Form, and the accompanying Loveswept cover notes, send your request and a self-addressed stamped envelope (Vermont and Washington State residents need not affix postage) before August 20, 1988 to the address listed in Paragraph 1 above.

LOVESWEPT™ HOMETOWN HUNK OFFICIAL ENTRY FORM

BANTAM BOOKS
HOMETOWN HUNK CONTEST
Dept. CN
666 Fifth Avenue
New York, New York 10102–0023

HOMETOWN HUNK CONTEST

YOUR NAME_____

YOUR ADDRESS_____

CITY_____ STATE_____ ZIP_____

THE NAME OF THE LOVESWEPT BOOK FOR WHICH YOU ARE ENTERING THIS PHOTO

_____by_____

YOUR RELATIONSHIP TO YOUR HERO_____

YOUR HERO'S NAME_____

YOUR HERO'S ADDRESS_____

CITY_____ STATE_____ ZIP_____

YOUR HERO'S TELEPHONE #_____

YOUR HERO'S DATE OF BIRTH_____

YOUR HERO'S SIGNATURE CONSENTING TO HIS PHOTOGRAPH ENTRY

_____

NEW!
Handsome Book Covers Specially Designed To Fit Loveswept Books

Our new French Calf Vinyl book covers come in a set of three great colors— royal blue, scarlet red and kachina green.

Each 7" × 9½" book cover has two deep vertical pockets, a handy sewn-in bookmark, and is soil and scratch resistant.

To order your set, use the form below.

THE DELANEY DYNASTY

where it all began . . .

Six daringly original novels written by three of the most successful romance writers today—Kay Hooper, Iris Johansen and Fayrene Preston.

THE SHAMROCK TRINITY

Heirs to a great dynasty, the Delaney brothers were united by blood, united by devotion to their rugged land and to the women they loved.

☐ **RAFE, THE MAVERICK** by
Kay Hooper   21786/$2.75
☐ **YORK, THE RENEGADE** by
Iris Johansen   21787/$2.75
☐ **BURKE, THE KINGPIN** by
Fayrene Preston   21788/$2.75

THE DELANEYS OF KILLAROO

Three dazzling sisters, heirs to a rich and savage land, determined to fight for their birthright, destined to find wild and wonderful love . . .

☐ **ADELAIDE, THE ENCHANTRESS** by
Kay Hooper   21872/$2.75
☐ **MATILDA, THE ADVENTURESS** by
Iris Johansen   21873/$2.75
☐ **SYDNEY, THE TEMPTRESS** by
Fayrene Preston   21874/$2.75

THE DELANEYS . . . men and women whose loves and passions are so glorious it takes many great romance novels by three bestselling authors to tell their tempestuous stories.

The birth of the Delaney Dynasty

Iris Johansen sets the historical stage for the love stories of the colorful founders of the Delaney Dynasty that continue in trilogies from all three authors.

DON'T MISS THE ENTHRALLING

by Iris Johansen

Scottish beauty Elspeth MacGregor travels to Hell's Bluff to hire Dominic Delaney to lead her to the magical lost city of Kantalan, but at first he refuses—the last thing he needs is to join a virginal scholar on a dangerous quest.

But Elspeth's fiery will coupled with her silky hair and milk-white skin prove irresistible, and Dominic acts—first with angry lust, then with a searing yet tender passion that brands her eternal soul and bonds them both to a heated and turbulent future.

Through wonders and tragedy, across the untamed splendors of Arizona and Mexico, Elspeth and Dominic draw closer to their dual destiny: to experience the dark mysteries and magnificent riches of Kantalan ... and to fulfill the promise of lasting love and the birth of a bold family dynasty.

☐ 26991 / $3.95

> "**SPLENDOR** is special—refreshing, riveting, fascinating. I loved it and hated to see it end."
> —*Johanna Lindsey*

- -

BANTAM
SHOP·AT·HOME
C·A·T·A·L·O·G

Special Offer
Buy a Bantam Book
for only 50¢.

Now you can have Bantam's catalog filled with hundreds of titles plus take advantage of our unique and exciting bonus book offer. A special offer which gives you the opportunity to purchase a Bantam book for only 50¢. Here's how!

By ordering any five books at the regular price per order, you can also choose any other single book listed (up to a $5.95 value) for just 50¢. Some restrictions do apply, but for further details why not send for Bantam's catalog of titles today!

Just send us your name and address and we will send you a catalog!